Puffin Plus
The Fortunate Few

Imagine the not-too-distant future and a world where four-year-old girls are sold to the highest bidder in order to train as professional gymnasts. This is the world of Jodie Bell, star of First Division club Shepherds Bushwhackers, veteran fourteen-year-old gymnast and a hard-nosed businesswoman.

In this future world, gymnastics has replaced football as the most popular spectator sport and also inherited the problems of violence and hooliganism on the terraces.

Jodie knows that by sixteen she will be past it, so she is determined to get everything she can out of her sport – not only fame and glory but also tremendous wealth. And if her pursuit of money sometimes means that she loses friends and makes a few enemies, so what? She thinks she can afford it.

In this wry and thought-provoking story, Tim Kennemore depicts a future that could happen all too easily.

Tim Kennemore

THE FORTUNATE FEW

PUFFIN BOOKS
in association with Faber and Faber

Puffin Books, Penguin Books Ltd, Harmondsworth, Middlesex, England
Penguin Books, 625 Madison Avenue, New York, New York 10022, U.S.A.
Penguin Books Australia Ltd, Ringwood, Victoria, Australia
Penguin Books Canada Ltd, 2801 John Street, Markham, Ontario, Canada L3R 1B4
Penguin Books (N.Z.) Ltd, 182–190 Wairau Road, Auckland 10, New Zealand

First published by Faber and Faber 1981
Published in Puffin Books 1983

Copyright © Tim Kennemore, 1981
All rights reserved

Made and printed in Great Britain by
Cox and Wyman, Reading
Filmset in Monophoto Plantin by
Northumberland Press Ltd, Gateshead

To my Grandmother,
Cynthia

I

Two days before her fourteenth birthday, Jodie Bell was sold for a quarter of a million pounds. She had guessed what was coming as soon as she saw her parents' Volvo parked in the drive – there could be no other explanation for their turning up on a Tuesday morning, and, sure enough, the summons arrived in the middle of Maths; Jodie Bell to see Miss Freeston in her office, immediately.

Thank God I didn't ask to go, she thought, hugging herself with buoyant triumph as she skipped along the corridor. It *had* been right to wait. But – *how much?* Two hundred thousand? She couldn't hope for more than that – could she?

Miss Freeston's office was in its usual state of frantic disarray. The desk was stacked with papers, files, long-forgotten notes torn from a pad marked 'Don't Forget', an overflowing In tray and an empty Out one. Paper clips dangled from a tiny magnetic pair of asymmetric bars, Miss Freeston's favourite executive toy; on the corner stood the much-coveted Manager of the Year Award, a six-inch-high replica of a gymnast on the balance beam, awarded to Dorothy Freeston, seven years earlier. Miss Freeston had a cavalier disregard for the honour and solemnity that went with this trophy; she used it as a paperweight, and a pile of ancient, coffee-stained receipts were stabbed on to the gymnast's outstretched foot. This attitude perhaps partly explained why neither Cheltenham Spartans nor Miss Freeston had won anything since.

'Sit down, Jodie, sit down. I won't keep you in suspense – you must know what I'm going to say. Your transfer was arranged this morning – you're a lucky girl, Jodie, you're going to the Bushwhackers. I couldn't have hoped for better for you.'

Bushwhackers – could be a lot worse – but *how much* is the transfer fee?

'It's the very last thing I wanted to do, Jodie. All of us here at Spartans are so sorry we have to let you go – you've been here seven years and built up your entire career with us – but you know how it is.'

Jodie did indeed. What about the money?

'We can't avoid relegation now, and the gate money is falling terribly. I expect you girls have noticed the empty seats. Next season it'll be worse. We need your fee; we can't afford to keep you. We'd be bankrupt.'

It was time to start saying a few of the right things.

'I've been very happy here, Miss Freeston. I feel like a rat deserting a sinking ship. It's hard to believe I'm worth that much money – however much it is . . .'

'Oh, Jodie, no! We're all so impressed by your loyalty in not asking for a transfer to a big club; you're much too good for Second Division gymnastics. Of course, you would have forfeited your share of the fee if you'd *requested* the transfer – did you realize that? – so I'm glad for your sake that it's happened this way . . .'

'About the fee, Miss Freeston . . .'

'Ah, yes – well, we had a few tentative offers from other clubs – you nearly went to Hampstead Heathens last Thursday – but Shepherds Bushwhackers came through with what we thought you were worth, and it's a fine club, Jodie – the facilities are first-rate, lovely new stadium, one of the best managers, and you'll be amongst friends, there are two other internationals in the team, you know them well . . .'

'Maggie and Liddy, yes.' Jodie's hands were clenched around the edges of the chair in an agony of impatience, and her feet kicked the air with frustration. Miss Freeston, behind the mountain of papers, was fortunately unable to see this. She began to rummage in one pile, and, miraculously, found what she was looking for almost straight away.

'Now, here's the contract. This has been a rush job, and we've kept it as secret as possible. You'll understand why. This is a wonderful day for you, Jodie. As of now you're the most valuable gymnast in the country.'

Jodie's feet froze; her fingers slowly straightened.

'Two hundred and fifty thousand – that's a quarter of a million pounds, my dear. So your five per cent would be – er . . .'

'Twelve thousand five hundred.' Oh, terrific, fantastic. Her Ralitex shares were creeping up beautifully, she'd have another ten thousand pounds' worth . . . Miss Freeston was looking somewhat taken aback.

'I'll take your word for that. Just as well, perhaps, that I manage gymnasts and not finances.' Considering the Spartans' recent disastrous record, it was highly debatable whether Miss Freeston ought to be managing anything at all, but Jodie smiled charitably. She could afford to be generous. She had just escaped from a sinking ship with a cool five per cent of a quarter of a million – Miss Freeston was not only being left to sink, if she didn't get the Spartans floating upwards double quick she would probably be sacked before the year was out.

'Obviously when the Press get hold of this you'll be mobbed; that's why we've hushed it up. Your parents are here now, having coffee with Mrs Burrows. They haven't been told yet. I felt you should be the first to know.'

Jodie agreed with this.

'So once they've signed the contract, I'm going to ask them to take you home until Thursday. Photographers and TV cameras are fun for the young ones, but distracting, and I'd sooner avoid it. I'm afraid you'll have to cope with the reporters on your own as best you can.'

Jodie would cope. She hoped that lovely Derek from the *Daily Satellite* would be there.

'By Thursday it'll all have died down. Go along now and ask your teachers for some work to keep you busy. I needn't tell you to do your training. That's all, then. I'll see you again when you get back. I want you in top form for the last match of the season. Cheddar Gorgons, at home. We might even scrape a draw if a couple of Gorgons sprain their ankles by Saturday afternoon.' She smiled affectionately at Jodie; Jodie smiled, and thought affectionately of her bank deposit account, building society build-up shares and index-linked Savings Bonds.

Jodie, like all top gymnasts, received a steady trickle of post, both at Spartans and at home. A small pile was waiting for her on the hall table; she scooped it up and took it through to the sitting-room.

Three requests for autographs. A letter from *Beam and Bar*, one of the worst of the weekly gymnastics magazines, a trashy rag of strip cartoons, picture stories, smudged photographs and cheap print that stained the fingers of its devoted readers. *Beam and Bar* wanted to know Jodie's favourite film star, where she bought her clothes, and other matters of vital interest. The next letter was more promising; Reid & Walker were launching a new breakfast cereal in October, and wondered if Jodie might consider putting her name behind the advertising campaign. Jodie pondered; she might, indeed. Food manufacturers paid well. She put this aside.

One small package remained. An autograph book, belonging to Emma Perry of Ruislip. Would Jodie please sign it? Jodie was Emma's absolute favourite gymnast. Emma had enclosed a stamped addressed envelope, which was more than most of them did. Jodie could never understand how so many people were willing to entrust an apparently valuable collection of autographs to the Post Office. She flipped through this one with amusement. It was a gaudy thing, a fruit cocktail of a book, pages a pastel rainbow of lime, orange, lemon and strawberry. Emma Perry had already sent it to all the major clubs; clearly she had a lot of absolute favourite gymnasts. Jodie found the Shepherds Bushwhackers team squad, squashed on to a lime page. She picked out a barely legible 'Maggie Carey' and a beautifully executed 'Gemma Liddington', rather spoiled by the last 'n' – Liddy had extended its legs downwards into the splits position. The other names were all familiar: top gymnasts at a top club. One of them was due for a rapid decline in fortune, however – someone would be dropped to make way for Jodie. Which? Liz Hopkins, Debbie Harris, Beth Laurence, Paula Michaels, Ann Pickford. She hoped it wouldn't be Beth, one of the very few people Jodie had any time for – a sweet blonde chuckle of a girl, human sunlight. Oh, well. It was their problem, not hers. She signed the book and sealed it carefully inside the envelope. There you go, Emma Perry. And don't come back.

'Jodie, the reporters are arriving.' Mrs Bell came in, wearing her habitual bewildered expression, and gazed with a mixture of doubt and desperation at the talented, brilliant stranger who had, some seven years before, been her daughter. Jodie, darling of the public, belonged to Cheltenham Spartans, to the Press, to the fans; to every-one but the Bells. From September she would belong in

London. She was growing more and more distant all the time; Mrs Bell was helpless to stop it. She had lost all control long ago. Was it selfish to wish that they had never allowed Jodie to enter professional gymnastics? Could they have stopped her?

'What should I tell them? They want to talk to you. I've taken the phone off the hook ... Jodie, you know I can't handle the Press.'

Jodie peeked round the edge of the curtain. Cameras clicked. Derek wasn't there.

'I'll wait till the others turn up. Otherwise I'll have to say it all twice.'

'But, Jodie, they're all over the lawn!'

'Yes, don't they look sweet? Like garden gnomes.' She picked up her schoolbag.

'What are you going to do now?'

'Boyle's Law.' She went upstairs to her room, mildly irritated. Her parents seemed to occupy only two dimensions; they were cardboard cut-outs. The real people in Jodie's life were those of the gymnastics world. Plus, of course, Derek of the *Satellite*.

By three o'clock Derek of the *Satellite* had arrived and was patiently waiting on the path, surrounded by a dozen or so gnomes, all clutching microphones, pads and pencils. Jodie brushed her hair into the slightly spiky Jodie Bell style, snapped on her sweet public-image smile and sailed out to Meet the Press. Her parents looked much relieved.

The usual inane crowd. 'Hello, Bill, sorry to keep you waiting – hi, Jeff, Pete, Marj, nice of you to come. And Derek. Good to see you, Derek.'

The gnomes surged. 'Jodie, how does it feel to be worth a quarter of a million pounds?'

And the usual inane questions. It was like performing

in a much-rehearsed play; Jodie had been word-perfect for years. It felt marvellous, she told them. She was very excited. She was over the moon. No, she hadn't dreamed of breaking the record fee. Yes, it was a great responsibility. Yes, the Bushwhackers were a wonderful club, she had always admired them ... This went on for some ten minutes. The eager, helpful smile did not slip for a moment, but as she went back indoors, waving for the photographers, it almost seemed as though Jodie winked in the general direction of Derek Holland, that very personable young gymnastics expert from the *Daily Satellite*.

Derek rang at half-past five.

'Well, Superstar, did I notice that quarter of a million pound eyelid twitching? That was a tip-top performance, Jode. As a gymnast you make a smashing actress.'

'You've taken your time.'

'Sorry, sorry, Your Royal Wealthiness. Did I keep you from your press-ups?'

'I've been training for the past hour and a half, thank you,' Jodie said coldly. 'If that's all you ...'

'No, come on, Jodie. I enjoyed the Shirley Temple impression, but if you'd like to say something interesting I'd be much obliged.'

'I might. If you take me out for a Big Mac tomorrow.'

'Going to treat a poor struggling journalist out of your five per cent?'

'I can't spend that till I'm eighteen. Otherwise I'd love to, of course.'

'Oh, of course, of course.'

'I'll give you an Exclusive for fifty quid.'

'Thanks, darling, but you've been transferred, not canonized. We can write a nice story from our file on you.

I'll pick you up at twelve.' He hung up. Jodie slammed the receiver down in temper, then laughed, against her will. She enjoyed Derek. Everything else apart, he was the only journalist not to have said anything about 'a ding-dong season for Bell' that year she'd had all the trouble with her arm.

Mrs Bell was watching the news on EECTV, the European channel, and looked up eagerly as Jodie came in. 'You just missed yourself on the BBC,' she said. 'You were the last item. Oh, look, there you are again.' After all these years, Mrs Bell still got excited at the sight of her daughter on television, and drooled over newspaper clippings. Jodie couldn't understand it. On the screen was the usual EECTV photograph, quite flattering, but a year old now. The spiky hair looked good; it was really rather attractive. She listened, not much interested.

'. . . smashing the previous record by twenty thousand pounds. Jodie's old club, Cheltenham Spartans, are currently bottom of the First Division of the Ambassador League, doomed to certain relegation . . . Jodie, now fourteen, was hailed as a future champion when she made her league début for Spartans at the age of eight. She was known as the "blonde urchin".' Cut to photo of Jodie's urchin days. She winced. 'At her Gloucester home this afternoon, Jodie told reporters that she was over the moon. And now, over to the studio, to our considerably less valuable colleagues for Europe Today.' A thirty-second report and only one mistake; they were wrong, by two days, about her age. For EECTV, who had once called her Joby Dell, that was really rather good.

Derek watched with amazement as Jodie tucked into her second Big Mac with relish.

'I thought you gymnasts were all kept on special diets.

How do you stay looking like a toothpick with an appetite like that?'

'I'm lucky. I stay like a toothpick, whatever I eat. Are you *quite* sure you don't want an Exclusive?'

'Yes, thank you, Your Right Royal Richness. Though our Battling Barbara might be thinking of doing a feature on you. She's been taking a great interest in gymnastics lately.'

'Who's Battling Barbara? Never heard of her.'

'Barbara Lloyd Purvis. Battling Barbara's her *polite* nickname. I'll tell you the others when you're sixteen. She's the Women's Page editor.'

'I *won't* be put on the Women's Page. I belong on the Sports Page.'

'You belong on the Financial Page, sweetheart, under a special heading, Goldmines. I know you, Jodie Bell. I've known you since you were eight. The little blonde urchin who captured the hearts of the nation.'

'You were the first to call me that, Derek Holland. I've still got the cutting. And you know what you were saying three weeks later? "Meet Kathy Locke, red-headed firebrand destined to be the new star in the gymnastics firmament." I've got that cutting too.'

'You know journalism, Jodie. The public like a new seven-year-old superstar every few weeks. They all fizzle out like damp squibs. You've lasted because you happen to be a superb gymnast.'

Jodie grinned at that, licking away her moustache of strawberry milkshake.

'So tell me your plans for your dazzling future.'

'Well, I was on the phone to Reid & Walker this morning. I'm to be the face that launches a thousand packets of Malties breakfast cereal.'

'Your *gymnastic* future, not the lucrative sidelines,

thank you. How will it feel, not being team captain any more? Will you mind being bossed by Maggie Carey?'

'I've been in the England team under Maggie, *as you know*, and she doesn't boss. I don't mind. Not at all.' It had not been inspiring, trying to gee up a team of mediocre gymnasts as they lurched from defeat to defeat. And Maggie was fifteen months older than Jodie, and wouldn't last indefinitely . . . oh, no, she didn't mind. Her prospects were excellent.

'So you'll be going on the summer tour of Eastern Europe with the Bush?'

'No, the transfer is for September. I'm a Spartan till then. We're touring France.'

'France!' Derek scoffed. 'Why go? Summer tours are optional. You'll learn nothing. The French have as much idea of gymnastics as the Eskimos do of camel-racing.'

'It's all practice and experience,' Jodie said primly. Camel-racing Eskimos would be much more entertaining company than cardboard parents, but she did not mention this; it would not look good, printed in the *Satellite*. 'Tell me more about this Battling Barbara Lloyd Pervert.'

'Lewd Pervert, is what we say. There, I wasn't going to tell you that till you were sixteen, you evil little capitalist. Actually, you wouldn't be her cup of tea at all.'

'Lewd perverts adore me, usually.'

'Don't be cheeky. No, her angle is the exploitation bit – poor pathetic little waifs, you know.'

'Exploitation! Do I look exploited?'

'According to B.B.L.P., you're being overworked and deprived of your childhood.'

Jodie laughed in scorn. 'I like hard work. I like gymnastics, I like travelling, and I like the mon . . . I'm doing nine O Levels, and I like doing those, too. I'll retire at sixteen, do A Levels and go to university. I've had a sensational childhood. And I'm – er – financially secure. Would you call me overworked and deprived?'

'No, Goldfingers, I'd call you rich. You're the exception, Jode. The one in a million who exploits the exploiters. That's why you're my favourite gymnast, and that's why I'm sitting here like a fool buying lunch for a millionairess. No, I'd steer clear of Battling Babs, if I were you. She asks all the old dumb questions, anyhow. Like: "What do you think about when you're balancing on one hand on a beam four inches wide?" – tripe like that.'

'Oh, bile.'

'Exactly. Jodie – what *do* you think about, balanced on that four-inch-wide beam?'

'The price of gold,' Jodie said, wiping her hands. 'Can I have another milkshake?'

2

Each of the Big Six clubs of the Ambassador League had a distinctive character in the minds of the public. Herne Bayonets were the current 'in' team – the one the celebrities went to watch. It was a good gimmick for a famous face to be snapped on the Bayonets' terraces. The life blood of the team was their manager, Rosie 'the Bionic Mouth' Fillmore, irreverent, outspoken and highly controversial. The Bayonets also had a rock star's daughter in their team, which helped.

The best that Potters Barmaids could produce was the grand-daughter of a Cabinet Minister, which was not considered an asset in the glamour stakes. The Barmaids sailed ever close to bankruptcy, and had just been forced to sell three good gymnasts in order to ward off the bailiffs. Bognor Rejects and Beachy Headhunters had been locked in deadly rivalry for many years; both teams went to enormous lengths to outdo the other. The Rejects had a little black book of dirty tricks; the Headhunters had just imported two Americans. Hampstead Heathens, League Champions, were a side of quality, respected throughout Europe, but had trouble controlling their supporters. The entire west stand had been wrecked in the 'Heathens' Holocaust' two seasons previously.

Amongst all this, Shepherds Bushwackers maintained an air of solid respectability. *Nice* people supported the Bush. You could take Grandma along to watch the Bush, and she would not be harmed. The three structures of the Bush complex, Academy, Gymnasium and Stadium,

were all purpose-built to the latest designs. Highly qualified teachers staffed the Academy; the Gymnasium had
been fitted with the very best training equipment; the new
stadium, rebuilt to hold an extra five thousand seated
spectators, was the pride of West London.

Jodie smiled politely as her mother kissed her cheek,
picked up her cases, the newest of which had a packet of
Malties emblazoned on each side, and made her way
towards the slender, dark, track-suited figure leaning
against the Academy wall.

'I'm your welcoming committee,' said Liddy. 'Beth
was coming, but I lost her on the way. Oh Lord God, I'm
glad you came here. We thought you would. Except
Debbie, who is anyway always wrong. That's a nice bag.
I'll carry it.'

'Courtesy of Reid & Walker Ltd. They're generous
with their free gifts. Nice bit of publicity for them, J. Bell
toting their tote bags. Where's Maggie?'

'Honourable Captain in conference with Honourable
Manager.'

'Honourable Gurney.'

'Honourable Gurney. Who will indeed be shortly
honourable if these rumours of an O.B.E. are true. Have
you met him yet?'

'I came up last week to battle out my contract terms.
And he showed me the new stadium. It wasn't finished
last time I was here, with Spartans.'

By unspoken consent the two girls did not discuss the
details of their respective contracts. A gaggle of seven-
year-olds rushed down the corridor, chattering; recog-
nizing Jodie they did a double-take and backed away,
goggle-eyed.

'They'll get used to you,' Liddy said. 'We're sharing a
room. I hope you don't mind.' It seemed that Liddy had

arranged things very well. She and Jodie had formed an instant alliance when, at the age of ten, they had both been draughted into the England Under Twelve squad. They had much in common.

'Do we know yet who's to be dropped?'

'Ah yes, we do. Liz Hopkins. She has signed her own death warrant.'

'Why? What's she done?'

'You will see,' Liddy said. 'You will see. What have you got in this thing? The British gold reserves?' She switched the bag to her other hand. 'This is our Common Room. That's what they think of us, you see. Gurney and Amey have a luxury suite, marked "Middle-Class Room". Now, Gurney wants you; you'd better go. Last door on the right. Today you will be a gravy-boat. Passed around from one person to the next. I'll take your bags to our room. Oh Lord God. What a weight.'

Bob Gurney was the type of manager invited to speak on television when the producer wanted a cool, reasoned viewpoint, softly-spoken, rather than the ravings of The Mouth. He contributed a great deal to the staid image of his team. On this occasion he had little to say to Jodie, having spent a gruelling two hours with her the week before, haggling over the small print regarding bonuses and injury insurance.

'Your academic records came through,' he said, running a hand through what little remained of his greying hair. 'I'm impressed. Nine O Levels – that's a lot to take on. I hope your gymnastics won't suffer. Even Liddy is only doing five. Well, that's all for the moment. Miss Amey and Dr Kennedy want to see you, in that order. You'll find Miss Amey in the gym and, some time this week, you must have a word with the P.R.O. I must say that I'm glad your transfer record was broken.' He shuddered delicately. 'I can't *abide* photographers milling round my office. We'd have been obliged to shake hands at least twenty times for their benefit.' Jodie's reign had lasted exactly three weeks; the Heathens had then bought Kerry Randall from the Barmaids for three hundred thousand.

The Gymnasium was eerily silent; classes would not begin until the next day. Jodie found Miss Amey, team coach, in the dressing-room, checking through a pile of leotards in the Bushwhackers' purple and gold.

'Oh, there you are.' She straightened and stood, legs straddled, hands on hips, nine stone eight pounds of solid, unyielding muscle topped by a bullet head. 'I want to run through your bar and beam routines, and see what weight training you've done. I don't suppose I'll get you looking like a Bush gymnast by Saturday, but we can make a start. Go and get changed. And don't imagine you'll be treated here as something special. You are *nobody*. You are *nothing*. Our squad is a well-oiled, smooth-running machine. We've no room for individuals at the Bush. One step out of line and I'll drop you like a brick. Get a move on.'

'You look rather pink,' said Dr Kennedy, nodding to Jodie to sit. 'Have you come from Miss Amey? I thought so. I keep a stock of Kleenex here; people in your situation are generally in need of them at this point. Now.' She perched a pair of dark-rimmed glasses on her nose. 'I've got your medical records, but we need to check a few things. Height and weight.' She performed the Weights and Measures Act on Jodie. 'Five two, six stone seven and a half. That's fine, ideal. Periods started?'

'No.'

'Good, then we needn't worry about the pills. Now,

breathe into the calorimeter. Thirty seconds. I'll signal when to stop.' Jodie breathed. The doctor measured her oxygen consumption rate, wrote some figures, went to the computer and punched buttons. 'You have a very high BMR. Quick metabolism. You'll need plenty of fuel.' The computer whirred and buzzed, rapidly printing lines of type. Dr Kennedy tore off the sheet. 'Here's your diet. Four copies; one for the kitchen, one for the office, one for you and one for me. And remember, no cheating. No contraband carbohydrate. The penalties are dire, I'm told.' She returned to her chair and her perusal of Jodie's medical file. 'Sorry if I appear somewhat brisk, but I have a dozen new six-year-olds to see yet, still at the sniffle stage, clutching their Snoopy dolls.'

'What's the average intake here?'

'We sign up anything up to seventy-five every year. There's a good deal of wastage, of course – only a quarter of those will ever make professionals. It makes financial sense in the long run, though. Sign them up when they're young, is the club policy. There's a very efficient scouting system here. Home-grown talent doesn't have to be bought for vast sums, like certain people.' She grinned at Jodie, who was nodding in approval at such sound economics.

'I suppose that's how the club can afford all this equipment, and the new stadium.'

'I suppose it is. Now – no allergies, no sleeping difficulties, and you're not on any drugs – quite remarkable. And your injury record is almost blank! How do you do it? Just this occasional problem with the right arm – oh, of course, your Shaposhnikova balance on the beam, you strained it . . . but that's all. Good heavens. When I think of the hours I've spent with poor Beth Laurence, treating that knee of hers . . .'

'I was born under a lucky star.'

'You must have been. Let's see, date of birth ... oh, you're a Cancer! Like me. Hard shell, soft inside. Is that you?'

'Hard shell, yes.'

'I see.' The doctor looked at her quizzically. 'Well, be sure to see me at the slightest sign of trouble, pain, discomfort, weight gain. We can't afford to have you out of action. More than my job's worth. A *lot* more,' she added, thinking of Jodie's transfer fee, and of her own salary. 'We have all the mod cons, as you see – that instrument of torture is a Thermal Treatment Unit, marvellous thing – Japanese. Mr Gurney's very hot on Thermals. Oh, good God, I made a joke. Well, if you want pain killers, sleeping pills, tranquillizers before a match, anti-depressants if things get on top of you –you only have to ask.'

Liddy was waiting outside, flexing her leg vertically against the wall.

'Did you see Amey yet?' She fell into step beside Jodie.

'I have had that pleasure.'

'The Mummy's Curse, I call her. I reckon that when she saw what she gave birth to her mummy must have cursed for three days without stopping. If she did not die of the shock. Did she call you a pensioners' outing?'

'No.'

'Constipated elephant?'

'No. Ruptured rhinoceros.'

'Oh Lord God. That's quite a compliment. She must have taken to you. Let's go and get our post.'

'As you know,' said Mr Gurney, 'last season we finished second in the Ambassador League.' The Bushwhackers sat silently on the gymnasium floor. They knew.

'You may think that's not at all bad. I wouldn't agree. I think it's disgraceful. Shall I tell you why?' The Bush-whackers waited for him to tell them why. Miss Amey stood, statue-like, hands clasped behind her back, face like reinforced concrete. 'Because you were good enough to win! You under-achieved! It's no shame to finish ninth, if you are ninth best. To be the best, and finish second . . .' There was a short silence. 'Well, we must put that behind us. A new season stretches ahead, and this year I want to see you where you belong. I want you to win the League.'

'He wants his O.B.E.,' Liddy said softly.

'So that is where we will concentrate our efforts. Last year we tried to cram in too many fixtures. So, bearing in mind that three of you have international commitments, I have refused all Friendlies in Europe.' There was a faint rustle of disappointment. 'However, I expect a good run in the European Trophy, which would mean plenty of travelling. And there is one outstanding fixture from last season; you're going to Bratislava in February.' This lightened the gloom not at all. Bratislava was about as exciting as Penrith; at least in Penrith the natives spoke English, of a sort.

Mr Gurney paused for a moment.

'He's getting ready for the bit about the jewels in the crown,' Liddy murmured.

'None of you can afford to feel secure. For each one of you who has made it into the team, there are a hundred young gymnasts straining every muscle to get your place. You have to prove yourselves in every match. You girls – you are the fortunate few. You are the jewels in the crown of the majestic sport of gymnastics. You may remain jewels; you may fade into nothing. It depends on you.'

*

Jodie looked around the gymnasium critically as the team did warming-up exercises, waiting for Miss Amey who was uncharacteristically late. Actually, not a bad lot at all. Beth was going through one of her brilliant phases. She hoped it would last. Debbie Harris, though – Jodie was doubtful about Debbie, who was sixteen now and unlikely to last the season. Like most gymnasts, Debbie had an old face on a childish body; from the neck up she could have been twenty at least, drawn, tense, tired. Her body looked tired too. Jodie watched a half-hearted tumbling routine. A clapped-out gymnast. She gave her a month at most.

'Stop what you're doing!' Miss Amey had entered the gym, silently. 'I've got something here for you to see, and let it be a lesson to you all. *Come on*, Elizabeth.'

'Oh, *no*,' whispered Liddy. Beth clapped her hands over her mouth. Liz Hopkins, her face beetroot, came through the door.

'What have you got on? Well? What have you got on?'

'My leotard, Miss Amey.'

'I told you *bra and pants*. You insolent little lump of suet. Get out there and change.'

The team stood wriggling awkwardly. Miss Amey's showdowns were calculated to cause the greatest embarrassment to the largest possible number of people. Paula Michaels had a coughing fit and glanced nervously at Miss Amey, who chose to ignore her.

Liz came back, a rounded figure in her underclothes, tears openly running down her cheeks by this time. For a budding beauty queen she had an excellent figure; for a gymnast she was gross.

'Fetch the scales. Now get on them. No, there in the middle where we can see you. Right. What do they say? Speak up, and stop slobbering. What do they say?'

'Eight s-stone two.'

'And what is your ideal weight?'

'Six eleven, Miss Amey.'

'Six eleven, Miss Amey. Step down. Well. What an obscenity.' She pinched Liz's stomach, rolling a fold of flesh between her fingers. 'Look at these thighs, everybody. Look at her. This is what happens when you over-indulge yourselves. Remember – you're all expendable. There is just one good thing about all this. We don't have to look at her. Elizabeth has been dropped. Not dropped to reserve; dropped altogether. And all because of her own greed. Mark it well. Thank you, Elizabeth. Go and see the doctor. A fine waste of her time, reducing a self-indulgent pig. Move! And the rest of you, start loosening up. Mr Gurney is coming to work on your vaulting.'

The girls moved silently into their warming-up routines; the muffled thuds of feet landing on mats were interrupted only by the sound of choking, hysterical sobs from the dressing-room.

3

In the Shepherds Bushwhackers pecking order the Public Relations Operative was rock bottom. His office, tucked away in the least accessible corner, had formerly been a storage cupboard. The lighting was dim, and the only source of heat an ancient electric fire, which didn't work. Its bare flex dangled limply. The Public Relations Operative was cold.

He was an earnest young man, fresh from university, where he had completed a three-year degree course in Sales Psychology, Administration and Human Relationships. He had written a thesis on Filing Systems; he had a particular passion for files. Apart from desk and chairs, his office was furnished solely by filing cabinets, filing drawers, box files and a computer, which was, after all, nothing but a very clever file. The blue file on his desk at this moment was that of Jodie Bell. Nothing he had read in it had quite prepared him for the girl who sat opposite him, scowling and silent. She would not be easy to relate to, he could tell. It would require all his training and expertise. He drew a deep breath, and tried again.

'So you see, Jodie, we have to establish your identity.'

'I've *got* an identity.' There was something about intense young men in horn-rimmed glasses that brought out the very worst in Jodie. 'Really, Mr – er – Byers – this is a complete waste of time.' She looked meaningfully at her watch.

Mr Byers battled with feelings of inadequacy. 'Oh, please call me Mervyn!' he said hopefully, remembering

Module 14 of his course – Balance of Power in the One-to-One Relationship. Jodie shuddered. 'I do understand, Jodie, that you already *have* an identity, but the thing is, it may not be quite the right one. You see, we have to decide how to sell you to the public. Take the supporters club – they'll be getting a message from you in the Christmas newsletter. And soon it'll be your turn to be Star Profile in the match programme. We have to choose your Bush Image.' He did wish Jodie would say something. 'Well, now, I've been looking through your file. I've unearthed every word that's ever been written about you, and all the interviews you've given, and I've tabulated and cross-referenced them' – Module 28, Data Analysis – 'and if you don't mind my putting it like this – you seem to come across as rather a tough cookie. In the nicest possible way, of course!'

Jodie bared her teeth, very slightly. Mr Byers gripped the comforting handle of his favourite filing cabinet, and tried to recall the finer points of the module about Breaking Down Hostility. 'So I thought we could capitalize on this, without actually exaggerating it . . . there seem to be two possible identities, Joker and Tomboy. Perhaps I should explain a bit more . . . the supporters like to feel that they *know* you, you see? So we feed them as much trivial information as we can think of, all consistent with your basic identity. Take Paula Michaels, for example. We've built her up as Trendy Teenager. We've made her a fan of the rock group the Raving Slugs.'

'*Rabid* Slugs.'

'Yes – thank you! Rabid!' A response! He was winning! 'We've photographed her in her bedroom with posters and album covers of the Rabid Slugs everywhere. And all the Slugs fans take notice – they remember the name Paula Michaels. They relate to her! It's that simple.

Maggie Carey – we gave her a Social Conscience. She visits sick children in hospital. Gemma Liddington – she's the Bush Intellectual – culture, and so forth. Strong appeal to the older supporter. And Beth Laurence, she's the team comedy turn – the Joker. Which brings me back to you. Can't have two Jokers – too unbalanced. You'll have to be the Tomboy. I think it suits you rather well. You know – a sort of *enfant terrible*.'

'I'm not an *enfant*!' snarled Jodie.

Module 46! Identity Reinforcement Aggression in the Early Adolescent! 'Of course not!' he said soothingly. 'Just an expression, you know. So will that be all right? Tomboy? We'll photograph you in sweatshirt and jeans, kicking a football or climbing a tree, or something.'

'Yeah, OK.' It was better than visiting sick children, anyhow.

'We mustn't go over the top, though. You mustn't appear *hard* – you have to be a sympathetic character. A *caring* Tomboy.'

'Caring about what?'

'Just *caring*,' Mr Byers said, shocked. 'Caring' was one of the first words that he had learned to use at university. Never once had he heard anybody ask 'caring about what?'. It was like blasphemy. 'Good.' He picked up another file, opened it and began to write. 'Now we just have to decide on an interest for you. A hobby.' He looked up with an encouraging smile, which was met by an expression of total scorn.

'I'm a gymnast. I thought you worked with gymnasts. You ought to know that none of us have time for hobbies.'

'Yes, but it wouldn't do for the *public* to know that, would it? You'd seem very dull. We have to *stress* your outside interests, even if they don't actually exist.'

'We never had any of this at Spartans.'

Mr Byers pointed a meaningful finger at the fixtures list for the new season: Cheltenham Spartans now relegated to the Second Division, the Bush one of the giants of the First. Jodie made an ambiguous noise, which he interpreted, more or less correctly, as meaning that he might, just possibly, be right, but if so he needn't think she was going to admit it.

'How about electronics?' he asked.

'Pardon?'

'Electronics. Goes rather well with the Tomboy identity, don't you think? Wires, batteries, circuits – that sort of thing. Can you change a plug?'

'Of course I can change a plug. But . . .'

'How about that, then? Your Hobby Picture could show you in dungarees, fiddling around with the inside of a television, or – er – changing a plug.' He gave a lifeless electric fire a hasty glance; this looked promising. 'Shall we settle for that, then?'

Hobby Picture – that rang a bell. Suddenly Jodie remembered what Liddy had told her about her own Hobby Picture. Liddy's hobby had been classical music, and the Bush had arranged a photographic session with the Sounds Unlimited Hi-Fi Emporium in Oxford Street. The manager of Sounds Unlimited had brought along a beautiful stereo and forty albums; Liddy had been photographed in her room, wearing headphones, surrounded by records, listening blissfully to Beethoven. When the session was over, she had smiled angelically at the manager, her brown eyes huge with trustful sincerity, and thanked him for all the lovely records. She would treasure them always, and would tell all her friends to shop at Sounds Unlimited. The manager had been so overcome that he had given her the stereo as well.

'I like Rolls Royces!' said Jodie.

'Rolls – Rolls Royces. But why?'

'I've always liked big cars. Tomboys do, don't they? And Rolls Royces are my favourites. You could take pictures of me sitting behind the wheel of one. I could . . .'

'But that won't do at all! You're not old enough to drive! We must be realistic, Jodie.'

'Oh. Well – yes, I've got it! I know what my hobby is!'

'You do?' Mr Byers was astounded. Jodie looked quite animated. She was taking an interest after all. He had made the breakthrough.

'Video Games! I love them!'

'You mean tele-football, that sort of thing? Yes, I suppose that could be a hobby . . .'

'Not tele-football, that's years out of date. They've got much better ones now. There's a new one, absolutely fantastic – Starship Voyager. It's got a complete control panel, and gears and steerage, and on the screen it shows your flight path all through the solar system, and meteorites and enemy missiles and invaders from other galaxies to destroy – and it plays space music – the President of the United States has got one. They aren't on sale to the public in this country yet, but you could arrange with the firm for me to have one – to have my picture taken with one – it would be easy. Publicity for them.'

Mr Byers felt uneasy. It was all so sudden. And yet – he had to concede that it was a very good idea. Such enthusiasm – it would come across in the picture, inspiring feelings of warmth and affection for Jodie in the hearts of the Video Game-addicted public. It was a masterly brainwave.

'I'll let you know the address of the firm.' Jodie got up. 'Videotronic, they're called.'

Somehow, Mr Byers thought, he had lost control of the interview. Matters had been taken out of his hands; the

Balance of Power had swung too far in the other direction. 'Before you go –' he began hesitantly, holding out a screwdriver – but it was too late. Mr Byers sighed. He kept asking for the handyman, but they never seemed to remember to send him. His fire would remain plugless; the Public Relations Operative would remain cold. Perhaps it would be a mild winter this year. 'Jodie Bell – the Caring Tomboy' he wrote, and closed the file.

The first match of the season looked like a cinch: Edge Hillbillies, at home. 'Don't get over-confident,' Mr Gurney warned in his pre-match pep-talk. 'Even the Hillbillies have to win sometimes.' But on this occasion the Bush easily outpointed them, to roars of 'Easy, easy' from the terraces. Clusters of Hillbilly supporters rallied with the first verse of 'Whackers for the Knackers', but they were drowned by the Whackerbacker sea of purple and gold. The team were jubilant in the dressing-room, having received a standing ovation as they left the arena. An excellent start.

'Sorry, everybody,' said Maggie Carey, leading a tall young woman through the swing door. 'Dope tests. This is Miss Peachey from the Ministry of Sport.'

There were loud groans. The blood tests were not so bad; there was a certain heroic nobility about baring your arm and standing, unflinching, watching the others wince as the needle found a vein. But there was neither drama nor heroism in the providing of a urine sample. Miss Peachey chose Ann Pickford, the reserve, for the blood, and handed the sample bottle to Beth Laurence, who pulled a face, but departed cheerfully enough to do her duty.

'Don't bother with the jokes, you rotten lot,' she said. 'I've heard them *all* before.'

Jodie, who was massaging her left leg, paused and looked up. She thought that Miss Peachey looked somewhat more approachable than most of her species.

'What exactly do you test for?' she asked. Miss Peachey was gratified by the interest.

'We check hormone levels, and for the presence of illegal steroids, certain pep-pills. You're Jodie Bell, aren't you? Can I have your autograph for my niece? And Beth, when she gets back. Beth's her favourite.'

'She's taking her time,' Liddy said. 'I hope she hasn't had a seizure of the bladder.'

'I really ought to go and select my victims from the Hillbillies,' Miss Peachey said, rising to her feet. 'I'll be back for the urine sample. Nice meeting you all.'

'We should be changing,' Maggie said. 'Before Amey starts bawling us out.'

'She is usually here, doing that, by this time,' said Liddy. 'Where can she have got to?'

Miss Amey was in the Manager's office.

'She'll have to go,' said Mr Gurney. 'No question about it. Thank God the girl's thick.'

'As we arranged?'

'As we arranged. Fetch her.'

'*What* is going on in here?' Miss Amey's voice cut through the laughter like a knife dipped in acid. An uneasy silence followed.

'You, Beth Laurence. As usual. Give that bottle to me. Well, here's a fine thing. Caught red-handed. I suppose you thought to celebrate your own mediocrity with a tot of whisky? Or is it brandy? Where did you get it from?'

'It's not alcohol, really, Miss Amey.'

'Then why all the giggles?' She shook the bottle. 'I'm

going to get to the bottom of this. And what's so funny about that? Of course it's alcohol. Would you be secretly passing round a bottle of lemon squash? Do you take me for a fool?'

No one had anything to say to that.

'Well, there's one way to find out.' She unscrewed the bottle. The girls watched, petrified with horror, dread and fascination, as she raised it to her lips. The moment seemed frozen, a still from a film. It was not happening. The bottle tilted.

'No, Miss Amey!' It was Maggie Carey, who was after all the team captain, and wished to remain so.

'Well, well. Margaret.' The bottle was lowered fractionally.

'Don't drink it, please, Miss Amey. You won't like it.'

'Thank you for your concern, Margaret. Can you give me one good reason why I should not?'

Maggie gave her one very good reason. Miss Amey's naturally pale face turned ashen. With exaggerated care, she resealed the bottle and laid it on the bench, turned abruptly and left, saying: 'Deborah Harris, Mr Gurney wishes to see you,' in a strangely quiet way.

Nobody was ever able to say with certainty whether or not the contents of the bottle had touched her lips.

'Now, Debbie, tell me the truth. How do you feel about your performance today?'

'Fine, Mr Gurney. I know I'm just as good as ever. I'm going to make this my best season of all.'

'I'm not sure I agree. I watched you very carefully today, Debbie, and you're slowing down. It's entirely natural. You're sixteen. A body can only take so many years of first-class competition.'

'But Mr Gurney, I feel so fit. I'm at my peak!'

'I don't think so. I must act in your best interests, Debbie. Another gruelling year – no. It could destroy you. Retire now, while you still have your health.'

Debbie slouched miserably in the chair, her lank red hair still damp from the shower.

'Retire? I hadn't thought . . . but I've never thought of anything but gymnastics!'

Mr Gurney tutted sympathetically. 'No. That's really rather a pity, you know. Have you never, for instance, thought about the unemployment situation?'

Debbie hadn't.

'Oh, Debbie. Four different daily papers are placed in your Common Room every morning. Have you ever looked at one?'

'Oh, yes, Mr Gurney.'

'Apart from the sports pages?'

'No, Mr Gurney.'

'No. Well, unemployment is currently running at 2.1 million. That's a lot of jobless people, Debbie. I should hate to see you join them. I've been looking at your academic record. There isn't very much of it, is there? Didn't you even try your C.S.E.?'

'I failed English, History and Maths, Mr Gurney. But I don't need C.S.E.s. With my experience I'll be able to get a coaching job somewhere.'

Mr Gurney shook his head mournfully. 'It doesn't work that way. Gymnastic coaches are trained experts, highly qualified.'

'I've saved a lot of money over the years!' This occurred to her for the first time. 'I've got thousands and thousands of pounds! I needn't worry about working.'

'The law forbids you to have that until you're eighteen. What will you do till then? And at the current rate of inflation, I estimate that when you do get the money it will last you at most for three years. Come, Debbie, don't look so distraught. I care very much what becomes of you. And I believe I can help. I've had a word with our chief scout, Pamela Martin. Pam would be happy to take you on as a trainee. Scouting is a fine career. Excellent prospects.'

Debbie wrinkled her forehead, trying to piece together the bits of the world that had just shattered around her.

'Think of the security. I would give you a signed contract. You need never worry about heating bills, the price of food – the Bush will be your home.'

'What would my salary be?'

Mr Gurney looked pained. 'Debbie, I think you've missed the point. *We* will be doing *you* a favour. We will be training you for a career. You must regard it as an apprenticeship. Strictly speaking, you should be paying us.'

'So – I'll be able to get a job later, with another club?'

'Of course. Go and think it over for a while.'

'No.' Debbie had entered the room with everything, one of the fortunate few; to leave it with nothing would be more than she could bear. 'I've made my mind up. I'd like to stay here.'

'Fine, fine. I'm so happy – I know it's the right decision. As it happens, I've got a contract handy. We can do the signing now.'

With some relief, Debbie wrote her name in round, babyish letters. Mr Gurney was glad to see that she did not notice, hidden in the middle of a dense paragraph of close print, the clause which committed her to stay at the Bush, unpaid, for the next seven years.

'Bill says John says we've lost Graham.' The disembodied voice crackled through a microphone above the studio. It was the latest of many delays. This was Jodie's fourth advertisement; she had come prepared, with *Jane Eyre*, and was taking advantage of the mislaying of Graham by ploughing through a few more dreary chapters.

She was not in the best of tempers. Monday's *Daily Satellite* had confirmed her suspicions; not only had Derek failed to report on her League début for the Bush, he had gone to Hampstead to watch Kerry Randall. And Kerry had scored a magnificent 9.9 on the floor; Jodie's best mark had been 9.8 on the beam. This had earned her a three hundred pound bonus, but all the same, she was not pleased.

'Hi. So sorry about this.' A gangling young man was standing beside her chair.

'It's O.K. Who are you?'

'I'm Graham. The floor manager.'

'Bill says John says you're lost.'

'No, no, I'm found. But Doreen says John's lost the continuity girl. What's the book?'

'*Jane Eyre*. School work. Not my cup of tea at all.'

'Oh dear no, mine neither. I'm a Barbara Cartland man, myself. What *is* your cup of tea?'

'Oh, thrillers, sci-fi, the *Financial Times*.'

Graham shrieked. 'That's a good one. Come on, Bill's saying Doreen wants to go for a take.'

Jodie walked on to the set and sat at the table. A bowl of Malties gazed drily up at her.

'Bill's lost the milk,' said Doreen. The make-up boy rushed on, powdered Jodie's cheeks, brushed her hair into Jodie Bell spikes. John found the milk, and lost Graham.

'Blow Graham,' said Doreen. 'Cue Jodie.'

Jodie beamed at the camera.

'It's hard work being a gymnast. I need packets of

energy to get me through the day. And this' – she touched the Malties packet – 'this *is* a packet of energy. After a bowl of Malties I feel ready for anything. And d'you know what?' She swallowed a mouthful, and allowed an expression of bliss to settle over her face as Malties and digestive juices made contact. 'They taste *terrific*. And, Mums – Malties are good news for you. They won't ruin your figure. Super toasted Malties contain just ninety calories in every scrumptious ounce. No wonder I'm a Malties girl.' She winked.

'Cut,' said Doreen. 'What do you think, Bill?'

'I thought it was awful,' said Bill. 'Jodie, you have to be convincing. You must take this seriously. *Believe* in your Malties!'

'I believe in the Malties,' Jodie said.

'Then where's the problem? Let it show! Think Malty!'

'Oh, it's no good. I can't. I can't say those lines. They're dumb. It's a lousy ad. Nobody would look twice at it. It would be better to film me throwing a Tsukahara over a Malties box the size of a vaulting horse. People might notice that.'

There was a deathly silence. Finally, Bill spoke.

'Graham, tell John to tell Ian we've got a rather unusual request for Props.'

Bill saw her to the door.

'A brilliant idea, darling,' he said, patting her on the back. 'I think we ought to pay you for that!'

'So do I.'

Bill laughed nervously. 'I was joking, darling. Well, I'll let you know the new date. A bore for you, but of course we'll be paying you for two days instead of one.' Jodie smiled.

'Have we lost Bill?' called a voice from within. She closed the door and set off into the darkening evening.

'So who is to take the place of dear departed Debbie?' Liddy wondered aloud as they trooped into the Common Room after lunch. 'Tracy Wilcox? Maggie, you must have some idea.'

'Nobody's said a word to me. It could be anyone.'

'Couldn't,' said a small voice. 'It's me.'

'Liz! You're back! I didn't see you there.'

'I'm surprised you can see me at all. I've lost so much weight I feel invisible.' Liz's face had fallen in, her cheeks were hollow, dark shadows circled her eyes. Her collarbone protruded cruelly.

'Oh Lord God. There is not enough of you left to fill your skin.' Liddy looked closer in consternation. 'How did they do it?'

'I've been on six hundred calories for the last fortnight. Under supervision. They told Dr Kennedy to hurry it up, that I was needed back in the team because of Deb retiring.' Her voice was flat and uninterested.

Beth perched on the arm of her chair.

'Six hundred! I can't believe it. Oh, poor Liz. You must have been starving.'

'I was on appetite suppressants. And actually, after a while you stop caring. I was just so miserable about being dropped . . . nobody said to *me* that it wasn't for ever.'

'Still, you're back to your right weight now. It's all over.'

'Yes. Oh no, it's not,' she sobbed suddenly. 'It's not. You don't know what I feel like. I've hardly got the strength to move. I feel half dead. Every time I stand up I go dizzy. I blacked out, once, in the clinic. How am I supposed to go out and do gymnastics?'

'But, Liz,' Beth said patiently, 'they'll put you back on to your usual meals now. You must try to forget about it. The dizziness will go as soon as you start to eat properly.'

Liz wiped her eyes with her sleeve. 'It makes no difference. I'm supposed to start some gentle training tomorrow. And I can't do it. I can't. I'll collapse. And then Amey'll drop me again.'

'What you need is some instant energy,' Jodie said. 'I wish I had a box of Malties I could sneak you, but I haven't.'

'Chocolate. That's the thing.' Beth sat upright and looked at her watch. 'Five minutes till ballet. I'll nip out to Bagnall's and get you a few bars.'

'Don't be a fool. Smuggling food to me – if you're caught they'll kill you.'

'I won't be caught. Milk or plain?'

'You're a lunatic, Beth Laurence. I wouldn't do it for you.'

'I'll get one of each. Won't be long.'

Liz made a slight movement forward as if to stop her, but was too late. 'She's a lunatic,' she said, in case anyone had not yet grasped this. Then she flopped back in the chair in a helpless attitude and began, softly, to cry again. 'Chocolate,' she sobbed. 'Oh, chocolate.'

4

'The Russians are coming' were the words on everybody's lips during the second week of November. This did not indicate that Soviet troops had been sighted scaling the cliffs of Dover; the Russian gymnastic team were due at Wembley for their annual display. They were in the habit of using this venue to experiment with new and ever-more-daring routines, and all seats were invariably sold out within an hour of the box office opening. Top managers, however, knew the right strings to pull, and Mr Gurney had a nice block of forty seats in an excellent position. Thither he took his best gymnasts to observe, mark and inwardly digest.

He was not the only one. Jodie spotted Rosie Fillmore, seated in the middle of a row of Herne Bayonets. The Bionic Mouth was closing around a giant hot dog, while the Bayonets, forbidden such luxuries, salivated enviously. And there were the Heathens, Kerry Randall prominent amongst them, the star of the moment. Jodie thought of things she would like to do to Kerry Randall's neck. At this stage of the season things were very tight at the top of the First Division; Heathens, Bushwhackers, Bognor Rejects and the surprise team of the season, Rhondda Valiants, were separated by very few points, and in some cases only by the apparatus averages.

The Russians, tiny, tough and gritty, marched on in perfect formation; a red flag fluttered high above the arena; their national anthem played. 'God save the Tsar,' sang Liddy.

'Quiet,' Jodie said. 'Plenty of room for a little one in Siberia. They've probably planted bugs under all the seats. Which one's Rostova?'

Everyone was asking that. The Russians had kept their more established stars at home, preferring to give the younger girls experience; the only big name present was Tamara Rostova, just ten, but already a famous and much written-about young lady.

Rostova was good. She was very good. Elf-like, she flew over the vault, swung effortlessly from higher to lower bar, pranced mischievously on the floor to the strains of a mazurka. But it was her beam exercise which really set the crowd buzzing – an almost ridiculous succession of balances, twists and somersaults, all rock-solid, never a quiver. 'She has made this apparatus her own,' scribbled all the journalists. This was the standard comment for such a performance.

'Did you see that?' Maggie gaped as Rostova executed a bewildering, dizzying dismount, gyrating wildly in the air and yet landing, with apparent ease, squarely on both feet. 'Did you see what she did, Beth?'

'Yes. Oh, help. Let's hope Amey missed it.' For this, the beam, was Beth's speciality, her prowess on the other apparatus being little more than average, and her dismounts were her strongest point – there was already a Laurence Dismount named after her. 'Nothing became her like the leaving of it,' Derek Holland had once written of Beth's beam routine, with some truth. Yes, there would be little peace for Beth from Miss Amey until she had mastered this incredible feat of Rostova's. She foresaw long hours of toil.

Whenever television cameras visited the Bush to cover a home match, the team was given a special lesson in TV

Technique at some time during the preceding week. This happened at the end of November, and the seven team members were sent along to the gymnasium with Mrs Chandler, the drama coach, on the Thursday afternoon.

'Quick bit of revision first,' she said as they settled down on the mats. 'You know that after the match an interviewer will talk to at least one of you, win or lose. Now, what must you remember?'

'Be a generous winner and a sporting loser,' they chorused, bored. They had been through this many times before.

'And?'

'Keep your eyes on the interviewer, never look directly into the camera.'

'Right. Paula, you be the interviewer. You've asked to speak to – let me see – you, Gemma Liddington. You've done very badly, Gemma. The Bush lost; you yourself fell off both bars and beam. Off you go.'

'How do you feel, Liddy?' Paula asked, brandishing an imaginary microphone.

'I-am-choked,' chanted Liddy. 'I-am-as-sick-as-a-dead-parrot. But there can be no question that at the end of the day the better team won. We were outclassed. We-deserve-to-be-shot.'

Mrs Chandler looked doubtful. 'Well, the words were right, but you mustn't sound as if you're reciting the Lord's Prayer. The viewers don't like that. You don't want them to think you've been coached. Be natural. Be spontaneous. OK, we'll try something else. Maggie, you've just scored 9.9 on the bars, and gone back to sit on the bench. The crowds are *roaring* for you.'

Maggie rose, ran lightly to the centre of the floor and waved, laughing and smiling, turning to face every direction.

'Yes, I thought you'd do that. You look too eager, Maggie. Mr Gurney has commissioned a special consumer survey dealing with exactly this sort of thing. The results indicate quite clearly that spectators like a little modesty. You must all be shrinking violets. How much better that would have looked if Maggie had shaken her head, and two or three of you practically *pushed* her up to take her applause. Let's do it that way. Again, Maggie. Remember – shrinking violet.'

Maggie wriggled bashfully.

'Good. Now, you others – that's the way. Fine. Remember – every viewer is a potential spectator and every spectator pays to get in. Audience satisfaction is money in the bank. Applause is coin-shaped. Now, I've got an old VTR to show you.'

Mrs Chandler went to the television and slotted in a tape as the girls clustered round the screen. The set flickered and showed a small dancing figure, clad in red.

'*Korbut*,' Jodie said with disdain. There were hoots of scorn.

'Hush. Watch.' Olga Korbut completed her floor exercise to the sound of a tinkling piano. Wild cheers erupted from the screen. 'Isn't she *marvellous*!' said the commentator.

'Isn't she *hopeless*,' said Liz. Mrs Chandler stopped the tape.

'Don't make fun of Korbut. You all owe a lot to her. Difficult as it is to believe, looking at her, that girl revolutionized gymnastics single-handed, back in 1972 at the Munich Olympics. What were the Olympics, Ann?'

'A sort of amateur do, every four years.'

'Right. And if it hadn't been for the interest sparked off by Korbut, gymnastics might well have remained a minority amateur sport. None of you would be where you

44

are today. Now. Why did it happen? What was so special about Korbut?'

They had been wondering about that. It was a puzzle.

'How old was she?' Maggie asked after a while.

'Seventeen.'

'Seventeen! Well, that's it then. It was like an old veteran coming back to Wimbledon. They were cheering her for still being alive.'

'You couldn't be more wrong. I remember the words of a commentator at the time – "How can you tell her that at seventeen she has the whole world ahead of her?" She was the baby! The youngest, the smallest.'

'Smallest?'

'Yes.' She wound the tape forward. 'Look at the others.'

'Oh, my God!'

'Exactly. But there was more to it than that.' She showed a montage of Korbut scenes: Korbut laughing, Korbut crying, Korbut coming to grief on the asymmetric bars, Korbut sitting with head buried in hands, Korbut triumphant on the podium with gold medal.

'Now *there* is where you can learn from her. Notice how she uses the cameras. Whenever she's on screen your eye is drawn straight to her. The public adored her. They couldn't get enough of her. This is what you girls must aim for. Know where the cameras are. One carefully-timed piece of charm seen on television could pay for a new set of weights in raised gate money. Well, that's all. I'll be watching on Saturday, and I want to *feel* your personalities coming over.' She switched the set off. 'Jodie Bell and Gemma Liddington, you're to wait here; Miss Amey wants to see you, with the choreographer. You're to have your music cassettes handy.'

Liddy grimaced eloquently. 'You lucky, lucky people,'

Beth said, skipping off. 'I'll come over later and help mop up the blood.'

'Oh happy us,' Liddy said bitterly.

'This is supposed to be our free time,' Jodie grumbled as they collected their music, Liddy's Chopin nocturne and her own Scott Joplin rag. 'I didn't think there was any problem with my floor exercise, and there's *certainly* nothing wrong with yours. Oh well. Perhaps she'll hand out fat cigars and beer cans, and we'll have a nice game of poker.'

'Perhaps she will show us her holiday snaps. "See, girls, here is Mother, jumping off the Golden Gate Bridge." Perhaps we will all four of us do the Charleston. Perhaps we should shut up; here she is.'

Miss Amey was followed into the gym by the Bush choreographer, John Phillips, who stood a full head taller. Trained in ballet, he had dedicated himself absolutely to the art of gymnastic choreography. He had written three books on the subject. John also had the unusual quality of adoring the gymnasts with whom he worked; he talked to them at length, drew out their personalities and shaped their routines in accordance with what he found.

Miss Amey had little time for John Phillips. Neither was she much interested in the niceties of artistic interpretation. Miss Amey believed in brute strength, muscle, power and guts. 'Guts!' she would cry, when a girl showed signs of flagging. 'Have some guts!' Liddy frequently remarked that she would like to have Miss Amey's guts, fried, on toast.

'I'm not happy with your floor exercises, either of you,' Miss Amey said briskly. 'Jodie, your routine is a farce. An absolute farce from start to finish. What's your second-choice piece of music?'

'A Hungarian dance.'

'Oh, Liszt.'

'Brahms, Miss Amey.'

'Same difference. Let's see the routine.'

Jodie marched mutinously on to the floor, waited for the cassette to start playing and performed the routine flawlessly.

'That was very nice, actually,' said John, leaning against the piano.

'It's an improvement,' said Miss Amey, writing notes. 'That other thing, that rag, might have been right for her when she was a scarecrow of eight. At fourteen it's a joke.'

'But everyone *associates* the *Maple Leaf Rag* with me. I can't drop it, just like that. I've always used it.'

Miss Amey glared icily. 'You are not the Crossroads Motel, Jodie Bell. You do not require a theme tune to announce your appearance. Perhaps you would like a fanfare of trumpets? Or the National Anthem, with everyone standing up for you? I've told you before what I think of that sort of attitude. You are *nothing*.'

'It's true, Jodie,' John said. 'The rag is too cute and young for you now. The Brahms – that was great. Jerky but with much more power. I'll work with you on the middle section, and polish it up a bit. You'll see I'm right.'

Jodie bit her lip. She could not have cared less about the music – she was sick of the sound of the *Maple Leaf Rag* in any case – but it was galling to lose a point to Miss Amey.

'Let's have a look at Liddy,' John said, anxious to divert attention from the still-simmering Jodie. Liddy signalled that she was ready. The first notes of the nocturne rang out like a shower of shimmering crystal. Jodie had seen this dozens of times, but still she watched. Tiny, lithe, graceful, Liddy moved like some unearthly spirit, throwing sequences of flips and somersaults, dancing, so perfectly attuned to the music that it almost seemed as though she were playing the notes herself; that the sounds were created by the delicate movements of her body. She told some poignant story, known only to herself and to Chopin.

'It'll have to be scrapped,' said Miss Amey. 'I've thought so for some time. You need something more in keeping with your image. Doesn't she, John?'

John looked uneasy. 'I must beg to differ there, Gill. I thought that was superb.'

Miss Amey took no notice. 'I want to see you doing something up-tempo, Gemma. Something modern. One of those disco-dance routines, or a bit of jazz. That would suit you far better.'

'Disco dancing,' said Liddy. 'No.'

Miss Amey's voice rattled like a machine gun:

'*All the black gymnasts do disco-dance routines!*'

'And I,' Liddy hissed, 'do *Chopin.*'

The two of them stood, glaring, eyes locked in mute hostility. The atmosphere was charged and crackling.

'Drop it, Gill,' John said softly. Miss Amey let a hiss of air out through clenched teeth and strode from the gym without another word.

John went and put an arm round Liddy. 'Don't worry,' he said gently. 'You stick to your Chopin. It's beautiful.' His voice tailed away. 'Well, I have to go. Don't . . . don't worry.'

Liddy stood for a full minute before joining Jodie on the bench. Her voice, when she spoke, was controlled, thoughtful, almost mild.

'I think perhaps what she would really like is to see me juggle with bananas and coconuts to the tune of *Ol' Man River*. My image, of course. How stupid of me to forget. White can be cute, dramatic, balletic, acrobatic. Black must not get above itself and try to be anything more than black.'

'This is a problem, Gill,' said Mr Gurney.

'Lucy Maddox says that her six- and seven-year-olds seem to positively dislike the beam. We have no up-and-coming talent at all, in that area. I wish I knew the reason for it.'

Mr Gurney sighed. 'Of course, you can't force them. Flair on the beam is something one's born with. Unfortunately our current lot seem to have been born without. Even in the team, it's our weakness. I thought we'd solved it by buying Jodie, but that's no more than a temporary answer. No depth – there'll be nobody to replace her. The only other beam star is Beth Laurence – exceptional, of course, but so unpredictable.'

'I've been working on the Rostova dismount with her for three hours a day, all week,' said Miss Amey. 'She's beginning to get it right, but that's in practice. Whether she'd bring it off on the day – I don't know. The girl has the wrong temperament. I've tried to toughen her up – waste of time. No guts. None at all. Might as well try to galvanize a jelly.'

'Mmmm. So, the situation is that when Beth and Jodie are finished we have *nobody* with the potential to fill the gaps. We'll have to buy. But we have just spent two million pounds on the stadium and re-equipping the gym.' He paused, tapping a pencil on the table. 'Gill.'

'Bob?'

'I think the time has come to exercise an Unborn Option.'

5

'Come in, Mr Gurney. I do hope Beth isn't in any trouble.'

'No, no. A wonderful girl. We're all very fond of her.'

Mrs Laurence smiled uncertainly as she hobbled over to the sofa and invited the manager to take a seat. She was still young, in her early thirties, and from a distance might have appeared even less, but closer examination revealed the lines which years of constant pain had etched into the smooth skin of her face.

'Can I offer you a drink?'

'Don't get up, please, Mrs Laurence. I'll help myself.' She frowned; after six years she was still not resigned to being treated like an invalid.

'If it's not Beth, what can I do for you? Don't misunderstand – I'm always happy to see you . . .'

'And I you, my dear Mrs Laurence. I often think of you here, and wonder how you are managing.'

'Oh, not so badly. This flat has good points and bad. Being on the first floor makes it awkward for me to get out, you know – I'm more or less housebound – but we get along. I'm just so glad that you found us a place so near the Bush.' Half against her will, she was talking quite eagerly. There was so seldom anyone to listen. 'Having Beth home at weekends, and some evenings during the week – well, it's worth all the inconvenience of that awful flight of stairs outside. My children are my world. I believe I'd have given up long ago if it weren't for them. Samantha's a darling, but still so very young –

at six they're still more of a responsibility than a companion ...'

Mr Gurney, sipping a Scotch, smiled sympathetically.

'But Beth now – well, she was a joy from the day she was born. A girl in a million. She's become my best friend. I'm so proud of her.'

'I can understand that. I take a great interest in Beth. And little Samantha. May I have a look at her?'

'Look at her ... yes, I suppose so. She's watching TV next door.'

'No, a proper look – could you bring her in here? I'd like to see how she's coming on.'

Mrs Laurence did not care to hear her younger daughter spoken of as though she were a piece of knitting; nor did she much care for Mr Gurney.

'No, I really think I'll leave her where she is,' she said, chin jutting firmly forward. Mr Gurney did not press the point.

'As you wish, Mrs Laurence. As you know, it was *such* a pleasure to me that the club was able to help you out after your husband's tragic accident, when we bought Beth. It is so rare, in my position, to be given the opportunity to aid a suffering human being, which you of course then were, being so badly injured yourself in the crash.'

'I owe you money? Is that why you came? But I was never given to understand that it was a loan. I can repay some of it from Beth's earnings, but she won't be eighteen for five years yet ...'

Mr Gurney looked shocked. 'Of course not, Mrs Laurence. The money was made over to you absolutely. No strings, no repayments. If you remember, you just had to sign the contract regarding our purchase and future options on Beth. And she shaped up so wonderfully well that naturally we renewed the contract on every occasion. Now, there were other clauses . . .'

Mrs Laurence was thinking furiously. 'Yes – that she should always be available for foreign travel – that I should supervise her diet when she was at home . . .'

'And that we should also have the option on any younger female siblings. That did not apply, since Beth was an only child. Now, I did not emphasize this at the time – Mr Laurence had just passed away and I had no wish to cause you further pain – but if you read the clause carefully you will see that it specifies that the siblings may be Born or Unborn at the time of signing.'

Mrs Laurence stared blankly at the wall. 'You never told me about this. Nobody did, Mr Gurney. Nobody told me.'

'Well, of course, it seemed totally irrelevant. Neither you nor I dreamed that at the time you were actually pregnant with Samantha.'

'You've come for Samantha.' She spoke heavily. 'Samantha!' she raised her voice. 'Come in here for a moment, darling.'

'I must disagree with your choice of words, Mrs Laurence. There is no question of Samantha being taken away. She may have no talent! At this stage, our only interest is to find out if she may prove worth training. And think of the future! Think how much more easily you would sleep, knowing that *both* your girls had sizeable fortunes awaiting them when they attained their majority.'

Mrs Laurence suffered considerable pain at night, and did not expect that she would ever sleep easily. Samantha, finger in mouth, appeared at the door.

'I'm watching the telly, Mum.' She eyed the stranger warily.

'I'm sorry, darling, but you'll have to leave it for a while. This nice ... this gentleman wants to meet you.'

Samantha sidled over and stood by her mother.

'Hello, Samantha.'

''Lo.'

'What a pretty little girl. I'm a very good friend of Beth's, you know.'

Samantha looked doubtful.

'Tell me what you like to do, Samantha.'

'I can read.'

'Can you! What a clever girl! And what else? Do you like to run and jump?'

'Don't do that. I play with my friend.'

'Isn't that nice! What do you play at?'

'Parties and schools.'

'Parties and schools! My goodness. And do you and your friend do handstands and roly-polies?' Samantha looked confused.

'She doesn't,' said her mother. 'She's quite different from Beth. You can see that. You remember how outgoing Beth was at this age. I'm sure Samantha will never be a gymnast.'

'Would you like to be a gymnast, Samantha?'

'No.'

'Well, you can't really say that until you've given it a try, can you? This is what I suggest, Mrs Laurence. Samantha can come along to a junior class twice a week and we'll see if she has any aptitude. We don't want to rush her. Mrs Maddox is a very good coach, all the little ones adore her.'

'Just twice a week? She won't have to go away to stay?'

'Dear, dear, no. You mustn't think that for a moment.' He was examining Samantha closely. 'She's a lovely shape.' He squatted on the floor. Samantha shrank back.

'Can you lift your leg, Samantha?' She stamped her foot. 'No, not like that. Keep it straight. Point your toe. Oh, that's nice, very nice.' He put a hand out and felt the muscles of her leg; Samantha gave a scream of indignation and buried her head in her mother's lap.

Mrs Laurence was white and angry. 'I don't blame her,' she said stiffly. 'I don't blame her. A strange man pinching her leg. There, darling, it's all right now. Hush.'

Mr Gurney got to his feet. 'I'm sure Samantha will do very well when she gains a little confidence. We'll be great friends then, won't we?'

'I don't like you,' said Samantha.

Jodie was sprawled on her bed, reading the newspaper. She saw that Cheltenham Spartans had fired Dorothy Freeston, and made a mental note to scribble a quick letter of sympathy. You never could tell when an old acquaintance might prove useful; it paid to keep in with people.

The main story on the back page was of course last night's international between England and Italy. Jodie skimmed through the story. There was a photograph, with her spiky head just visible in a corner, but the picture was dominated by the Peanut, as indeed the whole match had been. The international had been sponsored by a peanut manufacturing company with the appropriate name of Burbage and Salt. The entire gymnastics industry was heavily dependent on sponsorship; the Ambassador League was financed by a cigarette firm. Burbage and Salt had literally risen to the occasion by erecting a thirty-foot-high grinning peanut. The TV cameras had tried their hardest to avoid it, but with little success. Troupes of beaming Peanut girls had manned the exits and entrances, handing out free samples to public and Press, selling Peanut T-shirts, badges and posters, all

with the slogan: 'I'm the Gymnastic Peanut!' and, underneath, 'Buy Burbage and Salt'. Packets of nuts had also
been sent to the dressing-rooms after the match, only to
be collected and confiscated by the England manager.

There were many advantages in being selected for an
international match. All the gymnasts received ten tickets
for the very best seats, and Jodie had a longstanding
arrangement with Ticket Tout Ted – an arrangement
which had proved both convenient and lucrative for both
of them. Jodie also had the foresight to obtain a dozen
match programmes, and to persuade the whole team to
sign them – 'for my cousins, and my little nephew'. These
in a few years' time would be collectors' items, and would
fetch a small fortune.

Liddy came in with her post under her arm.

'Oh, the match report. Does it mention me?'

'Only the usual. "Gemma Liddington performed an
exceptional routine on the floor. She has truly made it her
own." I don't think anybody *noticed* us, actually. They
were all hypnotized by the Peanut.'

'And can you blame them?' Liddy began to tear en-
velopes open. 'Autograph. Autograph. Signed photo. Yet
another proposal of marriage from my devoted Bernard
of Bridlington, who still hopes that I will make him the
happiest of men, and is still prepared to wait for me for
ever. I'm afraid that is just what he will have to do.
Autograph. A letter from the Church of God Everywhere.'

'Who?'

'You heard. They wonder if I realize that God is everywhere, and therefore sees me when I shamelessly appear
in public with bare legs. They hope that I will soon see
the error of my ways, and save myself by seeking God
Everywhere. Oh well.'

'It's good to know that God watches the Bush.'

'You've missed the point. He's Everywhere. He's also at Bognor watching the Rejects and at Beachy Head watching the Headhunters. In which case I wish I knew why they have chosen me.'

'What's that?' Liddy had paused over the next letter.

'This is mine sincerely from my comrades Winston Royal and Vanessa Jones of the Young Black Consciousness Organization. They want me to join them in their fight for young black consciousness.'

'Will you?'

'I think I won't. I am young; I am black; I am conscious. Therefore I am already a member. I do not need to be organized by Winston and Vanessa to prove it.' She ripped the letter in half and threw it into the waste paper basket. 'Autograph. Request for a donation from the Animal Welfare Association.'

'These people ought to know that we can't spend our money, *or* give it away, yet.' Jodie received many such requests herself.

'When I'm eighteen,' said Liddy, 'when I'm eighteen I will send them Miss Amey, and they can attend to her welfare. What's this?' She perused a typed page for some time. 'Oh Lord God. The makers of Tenderwipe Toilet Tissue would like to sponsor me. They will use my name in their publicity and advertising, and every time I score more than 9.7 in a League match they will donate £100 to cancer research.'

'That's good for them, and good for cancer research. What's in it for you?'

'Five thousand pounds is in it for me.'

'Do it.'

'No. It would do my image no good to be forever associated with lavatory paper in the minds of the public. Think of the jokes. I have already thought of three.'

Jodie, who had only thought of two, grinned and turned to the City Page. Liddy's nose wrinkled delicately.

'That financial page is a mystery to me. Do you really understand it? *Really?*'

'Yes. Well – sort of. Well – bits. The bits that affect me. And when I get my degree in economics I'll understand it all.'

Liddy sat by Jodie on the bed.

'And you can handle all the profits from my School of Dance and make me very wealthy. We shall both be rich little old ladies together. Which will be one in the eye for a certain person who doubtless thinks that the only career open to me is to pick cotton.' Liddy had neither forgiven nor forgotten. She pointed to the page. 'Come on, then. Show me what is so fascinating in all that gobbledygook.'

'Well, you see here, the pound is doing well against the dollar and holding steady against the Deutschmark – that's good. And Ralitex shares have gone up by half a point – see the little $+\frac{1}{2}$.'

'I see that it's good for the pound, but what is good about Ralitex?'

'I own two per cent of it.'

'*Do* you?' Liddy was impressed. 'And what's this? Commodities – oh, gold, yes. Silver, wheat, coffee. Coffee? Do you perhaps own part of Brazil?'

'Not yet,' Jodie said. 'Not yet. Somebody at the door. Oh, hello, stranger.'

Beth slipped in and limped to the chair.

'Oh Lord God. Your knee's gone.'

'It's not as bad as it looks. Just a strain, I hope – I landed awkwardly. This is a Thermal Bandage.' She tapped her knee with pride. 'Brand new – Dr Kennedy was very excited about getting the chance to try it out. It's got tiny micro-electronic implants.'

'An electric leg,' Liddy said with interest. 'That could be fun. "Somebody plug Beth in, it's time for her beam exercise." I suppose that's what you were doing? The Rostova dismount?'

'What else?' Beth grimaced. 'Four hours yesterday and three today. Still, I can do it now. Usually. Amey reckons if I pull if off and the rest of the exercise goes OK, I ought to score 9.9 or 9.95, regularly. She's really worked up about it. Oh, God, she's been beastly to me, though ... All the same, you've got to hand it to her. She must have given up every second of her free time.'

Liddy snorted. 'Don't worry. She will have left herself plenty of time to dust her pictures of Hitler.'

'She *is* beastly to Beth, though,' Jodie said. 'I mean, even for her.'

'I think she wants me to scream back at her. Really. And I can't.'

'Of course you can't,' Liddy said. 'She expects everybody to be as vile as she is herself. She thinks vile equals good gymnast.'

'You know how she gets away with it,' Jodie said. 'She's such a damn good coach. I don't suppose anybody else in the country could have got Beth doing the Rostova thing so quickly. If it weren't for that, nobody would put up with her. So you'll be out of the team, Beth. I'm sorry.'

'I'm not,' Beth said. 'It's only for a week or two. I'm being rested, and right now I'm going home for a few days. That's what I came for – to say good-bye. Mum'll be thrilled.'

'How is she?'

'Just the same. She doesn't seem to get any better. I

wish I could be at home more.' She sighed. 'She doesn't say so, but I know she's looking forward to when I retire. We're going to have a party. Lashings of forbidden foods. I'll make up for seven years without chocolate ice cream in one glorious night.'

'You're getting really clever at rolling bandages, Debbie.'

'Thank you, Miss Martin. But I would like to try something else. I don't think I'm learning much about scouting.'

'You're only just beginning, Debbie! You can't expect someone to wave a wand and say "There, you're a scout." You have to learn all sides of the business of running a gymnastics club. You've hardly started.'

'It's been over three months.'

'And look what you've done in that time! You've sold programmes, shown visitors around, cleaned floors, taken Mr Gurney's lunch tray to him – you're doing wonderfully! Think how much you're learning. You've answered the telephone . . .'

'I could do that before, Miss Martin.'

'. . . and helped in the club shop on Saturdays . . .'

Debbie frowned. Selling plastic Jodie Bells and Maggie Careys was not her idea of a fun way to pass a Saturday afternoon.

'I still don't feel as if I'm being a trainee scout.'

'Well, I'll tell you what, Debbie. Next Wednesday evening I'm going over to the Bouncing Babes Nursery Gym in Putney. You can come along and see how it's done. Three top vaulters have come out of Putney; you and I may discover the fourth. And, Debbie – now that we're both staff, why don't you call me Pam?'

Debbie went pink with pleasure. Imagine that – she was on first-name terms with Miss Martin – with Pam. She was feeling more like a scout already.

'What shall I do now, Pam?'

'Keep rolling the bandages, Debbie.'

6

Jodie had a rotten Christmas. Every Christmas was rotten, but this one beat the lot. Going home was like stepping into a black and white television set, and the programme was one she had seen many times before. Her mother was still saying that all the political parties were as bad as each other. Her father was still saying that they ought to bring back National Service. Nothing changed. She ached for London, for gossip, training, skating with Beth and Liddy at Queens – though Beth's knee was still giving trouble and would not hold up to skating, she could be relied on to cheer from the sidelines.

The usual deluge of cards and presents from her fans arrived; there followed the annual ritual of trundling the gifts down to the hospital, accompanied by a reporter and photographer from *The Citizen*. It made a nice picture for her mother's albums, which now ran to eight volumes.

Jodie ate too much, watched too much television and felt terrible. Her older, married, cardboard brother had provided her with a cardboard nephew who screamed, yelled and wailed all through Christmas Day, roaring his disapproval equally at presents, crackers and his un-admiring aunt. 'Christmas is a time for children,' Mrs Bell kept saying, as if to excuse the din. 'To be shot,' Jodie added silently. The one bright spot was her Starship Voyager; she spent long hours shut away with it, engaged in inter-galactic warfare.

Frustration followed frustration. Her building society interest rate was lowered. On Boxing Day Liddy rang.

'I am hung over,' she said dolefully. 'Too much brandy butter. There was a very nice-looking young man asking for you, Jodie.'

'Oh yes? When was this?'

'On the last day. He said he had brought you a valuable present and I said what a pity, he had missed you by fifteen minutes. He was *very* charming. At first I hoped he might be Bernard of Bridlington. Anyway, he left the parcel. It's on your bedside table.'

'How on *earth* did he get in? Didn't he say who he was?'

Liddy hiccuped. 'No. Of course I looked at the label, but all it said was "to Fort Knox". Do you own two per cent of Fort Knox?'

Jodie could have wept. Derek. He had got in with his Press Card. Derek had brought her a present, and she hadn't been there. It was hardly bearable.

She rushed up to her room the second she got back to the Bush, only half-believing that the present existed at all. Such a thing had never happened before. How reliable was a tipsy Liddy?

But there it was. Oh, how gorgeous. She and Derek thought alike; he would have got her something she'd love. Her exploring fingers found rows of fascinating little knobbles. What in the world?

It was a small plastic cash register. In a fury she threw the toy to the floor; a bell rang and the drawer flew out. A tiny piece of paper was folded into one of the compartments. Oh – *just* like Derek. She forgave him at once. This was his devious way of sending her a message, he couldn't resist teasing at the same time. She pulled out the note, unfolding it with care and a growing sense of anticipation. A hidden letter – perhaps a secret assignation . . . It was Derek's electricity bill for the last quarter. Underneath he had written: 'See how the other half lives.'

★

'Hi, Jode. Glad you called. I was about to ring you.'

'I,' Jodie said coldly, 'grew out of practical jokes when was six.'

'Come on, darling, where's the famous Bell sense of umour? Don't look a gift horse, and all that. Very valu- ble trinket. From the Far East.'

'From the Far East?'

'Made in Hong Kong. Oh, Jode ... wherever did you earn a word like that. Listen. No, *listen*. I've got a scheme hat might line your already well-lined coffers consider- bly. Want to hear more?'

'I might. What's in it for you?'

'Enough to pay my next electricity bill, if I'm lucky. I ave a friend in the publishing business. Now, he thinks he time is ripe to bring out a gymnast's autobiography. ike yours. A really well-written one.'

'Meaning I'm to write it.'

'No, meaning I'm to write it.'

'Get lost. Why should you make money out of me, Derek Holland?'

'I'll tell you why. One, you don't have the talent. Two, ou don't have the time. Three, I have both. Four, Nigel vants it ready in three weeks. Only a journalist with facts nd files at his fingertips could produce an account of our brilliant and gold-plated career inside that deadline. Come on, Jode. Think of the lovely royalties. You'll get fair whack.'

'I'll see that I do.' Perhaps it wasn't such a bad idea at hat. 'Why all the hurry? When's this thing to be pub- ished?'

'April.'

'Don't take me for an April fool. Books take longer than hree months to come out. I know that.'

'You don't know everything, sweetheart. You're be- ind the times. New technology. The public likes its

books while they're topical. Nobody wants to rea
January's scandals in July. And talking of scandals, watc
out for Battling Babs. She's preparing to fire a broadsid
I should think they'll hear the cannons in Bratislava.'

'From what I remember of Bratislava, that'll be th
most exciting thing that's ever happened there. Goodby
Derek. I mustn't keep you from your deadlines. I'll be i
touch over the royalties.'

'This should be very interesting, Debbie.' Pam mad
a sharp left turn and stepped hard on the accelerator. I
was their second visit to the Bouncing Babes of Putney
Pam had spotted a likely four-year-old, well wort
another look. 'If Charmaine Francis is as good as she wa
last time, I might start to approach the Mother.'

Debbie was glad that she said 'I' and not 'we'. Th
Mothers made her nervous, and she didn't really fee
capable of approaching one just yet. Still, this beat rollin
bandages. Debbie was beginning to suspect the existenc
of a troop of Guerrilla Bandage Unrollers, sneaking roun
the gymnasium with the express purpose of plaguing he

'What should I do, Pam?'

'Sit and watch, Debbie. I'll be watching Charmaine
you watch the others. Remember the Four Point Plan
Balance, Fearlessness, Agility and Grit. That's what w
look for.'

Debbie nodded, pleased; she had remembered. It wa
like chanting 'thirty days hath September' ... or was
December? ... anyway, she was definitely learning some
thing.

It would be a great relief when she became a prope
scout. At present she occupied a no-man's-land, belong
ing neither with gymnasts nor with staff. It made for
lonely life, and in the evenings, in the solitude of her sma

room, she had turned to her old Enid Blyton books for comfort. It was reassuring to know that the Famous Five were still outwitting the combined forces of Scotland Yard, MI5 and Interpol; that Timmy the dog was still saying 'Woof woof', just as if he were human; that George still wanted to be a boy but had not yet achieved this.

The Mothers lined the far wall, fierce and frowning, lowering and glowering. Debbie sat opposite on a small hard chair and quaked. From her viewpoint the Mothers bore an uncanny resemblance to a firing squad; indeed, some looked as though they might well be concealing rifles under their coats. The Mothers hated each other, hated each other's children, scorned the teachers who foolishly underestimated the talent of their darlings, and distrusted the scouts. The atmosphere was slightly less friendly than Custer's Last Stand.

The Bouncing Babes bounced on regardless. They knew well what they would get from Mother, afterwards, if they did not.

'Not so *heavy*, Bridget. Be a butterfly!' called the harassed teacher. Bridget's Mother glared at her; the others smiled faintly. Debbie repeated the Four Point Plan, but when she reached 'Agility' all she could think of was whether she herself would be agile enough to dodge if the Mothers opened fire. Fearlessness, she muttered. Grit.

The session finished, and the Mothers marched grimly into the changing-room. Pam followed, her face set in a cheerful, friendly, Mother-approaching smile. Mrs Francis was tall, dark and muscular. She surveyed Pam through purple-tinted spectacles.

'A pleasure to meet you, Mrs Francis.'

'Doubtless.'

'I'm very interested in Charmaine.'

'So are lots of people. The Bayonets, Hillbillies, Heathens ... all we need is the Bushwhackers and we've got a full house. You *are* the Bushwhackers? I thought so. Bingo! We've won, Charmaine. Now we can buy Daddy a screwdriver and perhaps he'll put the kitchen door back.'

'Would you like to be a Bushwhacker, Charmaine?'

'Yes.'

'It's no use asking her. She says yes to everybody.'

'Well, we'd be very happy to show you around and answer your questions, Mrs Francis, you and Charmaine, *and* Mr Francis.'

'Mr Francis has a lot to do about the house. Come along, Charmaine, your left shoe goes on your left foot, which you'll find at the end of your left leg. We haven't got all night.'

'I wonder where you plan to go for your holidays this year, Mrs Francis.'

'Do you? Well, Mrs Didn'tcatchyourname, that all depends. The Heathens thought we might enjoy a fortnight in Biarritz, but the Headhunters have some idea about Rimini. According to the Rejects we're spending ten days in New York, *and* I'm to have a brand new mink coat, and Mr Francis a new washing machine. But, of course, we'll be interested to know the Bushwhackers' feelings on the subject.'

Pam hesitated, but only for a moment. Charmaine was a hot property. The Bush could afford to put in a high bid.

'I hear that a round-the-world cruise is a wonderful experience, Mrs Francis. And how long is it since you had a new car?'

'I'll let you know,' said Mrs Francis. 'Move, Charmaine. Daddy will have your tea ready.' They disappeared, watched by the other Mothers, who had suspended their inquests to listen to the conversation, bristling with silent fury and green with envy.

'Who's got the *Satellite*?' Jodie had become most interested in Derek's writing, since he had been appointed her Ghost. She had decided that it was no disgrace for one as busy as she to have her autobiography ghost-written – she was after all a professional gymnast, not to mention the O Levels. Of course, *Derek* would mention the O Levels. She phoned him at least once a day to tell him what he should mention, and, more important, what he should not. She was, in fact, haunting her own ghost.

'It's not here,' Liddy said. 'Maggie, have you got the *Satellite*?'

'Nope.'

'Probably someone's gone on strike, and there aren't any.'

'I haven't heard anything about a strike.' Jodie remembered that on the way to the Common Room she had passed Miss Amey. That was odd. The Mummy's Curse usually skulked in the gymnasium, planning the tortures of the day, until her first class arrived.

'I think I'll sneak out to Bagnall's and make sure,' she said on an impulse. The others shrugged; such enthusiasm for a newspaper was beyond their comprehension, but Jodie had many little peculiarities, and they were on the whole a tolerant crowd.

'*Satellite*?' said Mr Bagnall, 'I sent three, like always. Who's saying I didn't? I don't have to put up with this. I won't be called a liar. Who's calling me a liar?'

'Nobody,' Jodie said. 'It must have got lost. No – not by the paper boy. No, I'm not calling the paper boy a thief. Could I just buy another one, please? Thank you.' She slammed the door.

'The paper boy *is* a thief,' said Mrs Bagnall.

'That's not the point.'

Jodie stalked off down the pavement, highly irritated. 'No, I'm not calling you a pompous overweight bedbug,' she yelled over her shoulder. 'No, I'm not calling Mrs Bagnall a hag-ridden old witch.' She turned to the paper, flicking through it, saving Derek for later, and saw at once why their copy had been removed. *Blimey*.

She broke into a run, dodged through the side door, sprinted along the corridor and almost fell into the Common Room.

'We've been censored,' she said, breathlessly. 'Just you listen to this.'

It had been a most aggravating New Year for Mr Gurney. His name had been overlooked in the Honours List. In the very first match of the year there had been a most unpleasant stabbing incident on the terraces, and the Press had leapt into the attack with lurid headlines about gymnastics hooligans, and clubs who didn't take proper measures to control them. Fortunately the knife had not gone in too deeply, and the girl was under the age of criminal responsibility, so at least there would be no court case to follow. Also, her father was a councillor, which helped.

But now this. 'Free Our Exploited Children!' blazed the headline. 'Former Shepherds Bushwhackers gymnastics star Suzanne Dean today tells her shocking story to Barbara Lloyd Purvis in a *Satellite* Exclusive'. He read the page for the fifth time, noting the worst of the charges. Nothing that he couldn't cope with, but it was a great inconvenience, coming so soon after the stabbing. He had never liked Suzanne Dean. He said so to Miss Amey.

'Gutless little bitch,' said Miss Amey. 'It would have to be one of ours.' The telephone rang.

'Not the Press *again*,' Mr Gurney said wearily. 'You take it.'

'Bush. Amey. Oh – hold on.' She put a hand over the receiver. 'BBC News Review. Want you to go on TV tonight.'

Mr Gurney said a rude word.

'Hello? Mr Gurney is very happy to talk to you. I'm putting you through now. Hold the line, please.' She passed the receiver across the desk.

'Good afternoon. Yes. I see. A storm in a teacup, I assure you. I suggest you speak to Rosie Fillmore . . . oh. Well, in that case I will be glad to come along and put you right. Good day to you.' He looked up at Miss Amey. 'Apparently the Bionic Mouth wishes to remain firmly shut on this occasion. Right. Let's dig out some dirt on Dean.'

7

The Bushwhackers sat in an expectant circle around the television. Authority had abandoned its attempts at secrecy; it soon cottoned on to the fact that a *Satellite* was circulating, and, in any case, by nine o'clock the club was surrounded by reporters, all waving frantically at the girls in a vain attempt to interview them. 'No one is to leave the building!' Miss Amey thundered. Jodie yearned for a pair of 'Before' and 'After' photographs of Liz Hopkins; she could have sold those for a small fortune. She rushed to the telephone to offer Derek an Exclusive, only to be told that he had taken a holiday, in order to devote his time to writing her book.

'Gurney being grilled,' Beth said, hugging her knees, Thermal Bandage and all. 'Grilled Gurney. What a lovely thought.'

'A good thing it is the BBC,' Liddy said. 'We will not be in any danger of seeing Jodie leap over that giant cereal packet. I have *nightmares* about giant cereal packets.'

'Have *you* smiled the Malties smile today?' trilled Jodie in her advertisement voice.

Maggie was thinking. 'I remember Suzanne Dean, she was good. She left two or three years ago. Nice, quiet sort of girl.'

'Hush,' Beth said. 'He's coming on.' The room fell silent.

'... a most disturbing story which appeared in today's *Daily Satellite*. These are very serious allegations, Mr Gurney ...'

'They certainly are, and if they contained a grain of truth I should deserve to be thrown into jail. However, they come from a most unreliable source. I took a great interest in Suzanne Dean, as indeed I do in all my girls ...'

'I'm sure you did, but ...'

'... and the sad truth is that she never really was a first class gymnast. These spiteful little attacks invariably come from girls who blame the club for their own lack of talent. Suzanne always had many problems. Her mother's third husband ...'

'With respect, we aren't really interested in your opinion of Suzanne. We would like to know how you answer her charges. For instance, she accuses you of cradle-snatching. I quote: "Children are bought from their parents before they are five years old, and from then on are seen as nothing more than property to be exploited to make money for the clubs."'

'I assure you that it is the girls themselves who make the money. The law is strict about this. Their earnings – which are considerable – are invested for them. A wonderful start to a young life. I often tell my girls that they are the fortunate few. If Suzanne truly has no money then I'm afraid she has squandered her savings foolishly. And of course girls are not "bought from their parents". This is illegal. No payments are ever made to parents.'

'But, Mr Gurney, surely you appreciate the public's concern over the fact that it is easy to manipulate these children simply because of their age. How can a child of five understand the meaning of signing a contract?'

'The parents countersign all contracts. It is not our policy, in any case, to allow a girl to sign professional forms until she is nine, by which time she will have been training for some years, and has a good understanding of what lies ahead. The girl and the parents decide. There is no question of coercion. That would be criminal. I am not a crook.'

'I'd like to move on to the most serious points, Mr Gurney – those dealing with starvation and drugs. To take the first of those – Suzanne claims that she and her team-mates were not only kept on rigid diets, they were actually *starved* if necessary, to keep them underweight.'

Mr Gurney allowed a gentle smile to flicker over his face.

'If by rigid diets you mean high-protein diets, diets lacking in sugary goo, I must say yes. And if parents everywhere copied this we would have a nation of healthy children. I must plead guilty to the charge of not ruining the girls' teeth.'

'But the question of weight . . .'

'A gymnast is solid muscle. They look small, but they're built like battering rams. The combination of sensible food and their training schedules makes them the fittest, healthiest young people in the country. Can you object to that? They require, and *get*, plenty of nourishing food to replace the energy they burn. Our computer calculates an ideal diet for each individual girl.'

'But if they are given drugs on a regular basis . . .'

'As you know, the Ministry of Sport performs spot-checks. No illegal substances have ever been found. Remember that it is the Government, not I, that decides which drugs are permitted and which are not. We never give the least medication without careful thought. Health is a prior concern. We employ a doctor whose full-time job is the medical welfare of the girls.'

'Finally, I would like to bring up Suzanne's point about education. She left you without qualifications, virtually unemployable. Surely these young girls are being deprived of academic opportunities?'

'That is a comment on Suzanne, not on the Bush. Like all clubs, we have an Academy staffed by the most highly-qualified teachers . . .'

'You're evading the question. What use are qualified teachers, if the girls have to spend all their time sweating in the gym?'

'The timetable provides for the fullest of academic courses. The *Daily Satellite* is very welcome to publish one. Gymnasts have a broad education, stretching far beyond the classroom desk. They travel widely; my team has been to Japan, Latin America, Canada, all over Europe. I have girls who can say "I am as sick as a dead dog" in Rumanian, and "the better team won at the end of the day" in Greek. We travel as a happy family. The Bush is *run* like a happy family. I like to think that I serve as a father figure to the girls. My coach, Miss Amey, is their mother-substitute. It's so charming to see them running to her with their little problems.' He smiled sentimentally. The interviewer looked slightly sick.

'I'd like to take this further, Mr Gurney, but we've come to the end of our time. Back to Jill at the news desk.'

Beth switched off. 'That was priceless. At one point he almost had *me* believing him.'

Liddy had collapsed and was still shaking with laughter. 'Oh dear,' she gasped, holding her sides. 'Oh dear dear dear. I must remember to run to Substitute-Mother Amey and tell her my little problem. I keep wanting to set fire to her. Oh Lord God.'

'She's off again.' Jodie was giggling too; Liddy could be very infectious. 'What is it now?'

'The ... Substitute-Mummy's Curse,' spluttered Liddy. 'Oh Lord God. I am ruptured.'

Mr Gurney was proved right; the Suzanne Dean Revelations were no more than a storm in a teacup, and a storm which blew over very quickly. There were letters to the Press, and mild rumblings that Someone Ought to Look Into It, but the letters were soon forgotten, and nobody did. The media tried valiantly to persuade Suzanne to launch a counterattack, but Miss Amey had traced her and paid her a visit, and Suzanne remained silent.

However, a star of ill-omen seemed to be cursing the Bush. Nothing exactly disastrous happened; it was more a series of minor irritations, proving the law that if a thing can go wrong, it will. An urgently needed consignment of new leotards went astray in the post, inexplicably turning up in Aberdeen three weeks later. Maggie Carey was nominated as BBC Sportswoman of the Year, and lost. Gemma Liddington was nominated as *Evening Star* Sports Personality of the Year, and lost. Beth Laurence's knee injury dragged on, her absence from the team meaning the probable loss of several points in every match. Charmaine Francis went to the Heathens, and her parents moved into a beautiful detached house in Hampstead. Jodie Bell's Ralitex shares began to fall; the Public Relations Operative developed chilblains.

Then there was the business of foreign travel. The first two rounds of the European Trophy had taken the Bushwhackers to Reykjavik and Rotterdam. It was worse than Bratislava. Even Bratislava brought unforeseen problems; the Supporters Club, the Whackerbackers, anxious not to miss the Friendly, chartered an aeroplane. Mr Gurney groaned deeply when he heard this. 'There won't be a seat left intact by the time they get to Czechoslovakia.' Again, he was proved right.

They waited in suspense for news of the third round of the Trophy. Italy? France? Spain? Sadly not. They were drawn against the only other English club left in the contest. Bognor Rejects. It was a cruel blow.

The streets of Bognor were lined by hordes of shrieking girls wearing hats and scarves in Reject red and green. The Bush team coach was pelted with rotten fruit and vegetables as it tried to drive to the stadium. 'BUSH OFF!' read the banners. 'NARF OFF WHACKERS.' One said 'GURNEY WASHES WHITER', which was so subtle that nobody understood it. 'Murder them!' yelled the crowds. It was the usual Bognor welcome, magnified ten times. Mr Gurney requested police protection. Arrests were made, and Bognor Police Station was soon overflowing with a militant nine-year-old army. Away matches at Bognor were never easy.

Ann Pickford, usually reserve but currently standing in for Beth in the team, was the weak link in the Bush chain. Despite the police cordon, between the coach and the stadium door a Reject supporter managed to break through, and bit her in the leg. Though not seriously hurt she was much shaken; she performed like an idiot, and the Bush were defeated by a substantial margin of 6.5 points. They would have to produce something very special in the second leg of the tie, if they were to avoid what would be a catastrophic defeat.

'Jodie – good to meet you at last. I'm Nigel Pinder, I'm the editor – this is Sally Smith, who's masterminding the publicity campaign. Derek Holland – oh, of course you know Derek.'

'My spook.' Jodie sat down.

'*Ghost*,' said Derek. 'Well, the book's finished, Jode, and Nigel's given it the thumbs up.'

'When do I get to read it?'

'Now,' Nigel said. 'Take a copy with you when you go. You're supposed to have written the thing, after all. We must remember that.'

Jodie reached for the manuscript and glanced at the top page.

'Chapter One – "In the Beginning". Oh, I like that, Derek. In the beginning there was darkness on the face of the void and God created Jodie Bell.'

'Everyone makes mistakes, darling.'

'Where did you get all this about my childhood?'

'From your parents. I've been to see them. It's called research.'

'*Have* you? What did they say?'

'Not a lot. Your father kept muttering that if I'd done my National Service I shouldn't have this disgusting long hair. Actually, I had to make most of it up, but don't worry, it all fits your saintly image to a T.'

'What about a title?' Nigel asked. 'A nice little pun, perhaps. Let's see. Bell. Jodie. I know – Bellissima. Italian. Very beautiful.'

'Dumb-Bell,' said Derek. 'English. Thick.'

'Holland,' flared Jodie. 'Dutch. Pathetic.' Nigel and Sally looked uneasy; Derek grinned, Jodie glared.

'I thought of calling it *Jodie*,' Derek said.

'Oh, I like that. Nice and uncomplicated. Straight to the point. *Jodie!* with an exclamation mark.'

'No exclamation mark,' said Derek. 'She *is* the exclamation mark.'

Nigel looked at Sally. Sally agreed with Derek. The exclamation mark went.

'This is a marvellous time to bring the book out,' Nigel

said. 'Jodie's name has never been bigger, what with the success of the Malties campaign. I love the little Jodie picture cards in the packets. I wonder who thought that one up.'

'I did,' said Jodie. She was seriously considering going into advertising, once she had her degree.

'Good for you. My mother's got the whole set. They sit in a row on the breakfast table.'

'All sorts of comments come to mind,' Derek said, 'but I'll restrain myself. What are the campaign plans, Sal?'

'I've thought of a lovely stunt. That four-inch beam fascinates people; they always wonder what it's like up there. So we're rigging up a beam, and anyone who walks across it gets the book for half price.'

'What do I do?' Jodie asked. 'Catch them as they fall off?'

'You'll be at the other end, signing the books. Here's the clever bit – I've devised a one-way system. Once in, you can't get out. Either you cross the beam and pay half price, or you don't cross it and you pay full price. We can't lose. I've arranged for you to appear on local and national radio, and we're putting ads in the papers.'

'It'll do for a start,' Nigel said. 'Where's this beam business going to happen?'

'Trial run at the Readers Revenge Bookstore in Brent Cross. They're having a Jodie Bell Day. If it's a success we'll transfer her to the West End.'

'Fine. Well, thanks for coming, Jodie. Now off you go and read what you've written. I really think we've got all the ingredients for a best-seller here.'

'Money comes to money,' said Derek. 'And the rich get richer.'

8

At a corner table in Bert's Bistro, Debbie took a minute sip from her glass of Seven-Up, and doodled with a red biro on the back of an old, unsold programme. Debbie was the person who hadn't sold it. Every Saturday Pam gave her a pep talk on Sales Technique, but somehow Debbie could never get rid of as many programmes as the other sellers did. It was never easy for her to switch on a welcoming, helpful smile and approach the nastier variety of Whackerbacker – particularly the ones with chains and padlocks swinging from their ears. They weren't so bad once they started at secondary school and began to take an interest in boys.

Debbie liked to draw hearts. She had already drawn a long line of them; now she began to convert this into a whole network, a grid of interlocking hearts. She coloured some in red, found a blue biro in her pocket and coloured others in blue. Then she enclosed the whole thing in a giant letter D. It looked very good, she thought. It was full of hidden meanings. Debbie could never understand why she hadn't been allowed to try her O Level Art, when she could draw hearts so well.

The Seven-Up was by now quite flat; she had made it last for nearly forty minutes. Her record was an hour and a quarter. All sorts of strange and lonely people came to Bert's, and seldom were they in a hurry to go. Bert didn't seem to mind. In the opposite corner, an old man was stirring his tea with his dentures, specifically removed for the purpose. As Debbie watched, he snapped them back in his mouth and began, morosely, to drink.

'Mind if I share your table?'

Debbie jumped. 'What? No.' A stocky, ginger-haired man slid into the seat opposite her, and set down a cup containing a pale brown liquid, heavy with powdered milk. This was coffee à la Bert. The man took a cautious sip. He looked rather familiar; Debbie tried to think where she might have seen him before.

'Isn't it terrible?' he said, with a friendly conspiratorial grin, as if only he and she, in all the world, knew precisely the degree of terribleness of Bert's coffee. He dropped four lumps of sugar into the cup. 'Best to drown the taste. My *God!* Is it?'

'I should think so,' Debbie said, 'unless it's tea. You can't always tell.'

'Not that! You. Debbie Harris, isn't it? No – I don't need to ask. I know you. Every week I used to watch you at the Bush. Terrific gymnast. Superb. Whatever happened to you?'

'I've retired.' Debbie was trying very hard not to blush.

'Retired? But that's criminal. You were just at your peak!'

'I know!' Debbie sat bolt upright. 'I told Mr Gurney that! He didn't listen. He just went on about unemployment and inflation.'

'It's outrageous. Those vaults of yours! Poetry. They were sonnets in mid-air.'

'They were piked Tsukaharas, usually,' Debbie said doubtfully. 'Do you work in gymnastics, then?'

'What? Good Lord, no. Did I say that? No – but you could say I'm interested. Thinking of writing a book, actually. About gymnastics technique, you know. Tony James is the name. Look – if you're really not performing any more – and it's a wicked waste – how about helping me out? You could be my technical adviser. I'll pay you, of course.'

Debbie gazed at him in silence. She could not believe what she was hearing. She had been so very unhappy, and now suddenly here was somebody offering to take her away from it all. He thought she was wonderful – he had said so. She leaned forward and prepared to open her heart to him.

'Can I really? It's so rotten, what I'm doing at the Bush. I'm never going to be any good at scouting. I hate it. I don't even get paid. They don't . . .'

'Hang on, hang on. You say you're still at the Bush? Working there?'

'Yes, but it doesn't matter! I . . .'

'Have you signed a contract?'

'Oh. Yes, I did. Oh dear. But – oh.'

'You didn't tell me that, did you? Come on, don't look like that. Oh, please don't cry. Look, there's no reason why you shouldn't stay at the Bush *and* earn a bit of pocket-money working for me, is there?'

Debbie dabbed bleakly at her eyes with a tissue. 'Isn't there?'

'Course not. Tell you what. I've taken a special interest in the cup tie against Bognor Rejects – I'm thinking of doing a sort of thesis about it – and you could really help me there. You must spend a lot of time around the gymnasts while they're training – you know what's going on. What I'd like to know is what sort of tactics they intend to use for the second leg of the tie. Any new techniques, unusual moves, any particular problems they're having – you know the kind of thing I mean. It would be terribly relevant to my book, you see.'

'Oh. All right.' Debbie's head reeled with disappointment; she was hardly listening. She had found a rescuer, and now it seemed that she was unrescuable. There was no way out.

'Here's my phone number.' Tony scribbled on a note-pad, tore the sheet out and handed it over. 'Just give me a ring any time before the match. I'll pay you whatever it's worth. OK?'

'OK.' She glanced down, and saw that it was a Bognor number. That was funny. You'd think he'd study the Rejects, not the Bush, if he lived in Bognor.

'Chin up!' Tony said kindly. 'Well – I have to dash. Bye!'

'Bye.' Debbie had the feeling that there was something here she didn't quite understand. As he pushed the door open and walked out, whistling cheerfully, she wondered again why it was that his face seemed to ring a distant bell. But it was not in Debbie's nature to wonder about any-thing for long, so she never realized that he was in fact an assistant coach at Bognor, and that she had seen him, several times, rushing with anaesthetic and bandages to the aid of an injured Reject. She turned the piece of paper over, sipped her Seven-Up, and began to draw hearts. Very soon she had forgotten all about it. From Bert's radio there rose the sound of a solitary saxophone, melan-choly dusk music; the lonely people sat, and sipped, and listened.

'Guess what.'
'What, Beth?'
'Miss Amey says I'm OK to compete. I'm back in the team!'

The atmosphere in the dressing-room brightened per-ceptibly. They were all aware that the run of bad luck had dated, more or less, from the time of Beth's injury. Her return ought by the same token to be the turning point. They would have their vengeance over Bognor. Ann Pickford looked happier than anybody. She had not been looking forward to this second confrontation with the Rejects.

Jodie prodded the knee experimentally.

'All that electric implant business, waste of good money. I've never known an injury to drag on so. Do you really feel a hundred per cent fit?'

'Well – ninety-eight. I hope I'm drawn to go on the beam first. I'll be happier when I've got the Rostova over.'

Beth was drawn to go on the beam last. Jodie, one rotation behind her, watched closely as Beth did her floor exercise, a vivacious and spirited performance to the music of *Nut Rocker*. The knee, tightly bandaged, showed no signs of weakness. The crowd went wild – 'Welcome back, welcome back,' they chanted, swaying rhythmically from side to side. Beth Laurence was highly popular among the Whackerbackers; they had missed her.

The gymnasts moved round, and moved round again. The electronic scoreboard computed and flashed the running totals: Bushwhackers 102, Rejects 97.5. A lead of seven clear points was needed if the Bush were to go through to the fourth round. Miss Amey bawled abuse from the sidelines.

Jodie tried to forget that Derek was watching from the Press box. Normally she was glad to see him; today she was unaccountably nervous. She performed two competent vaults, scoring 9.45, and sat down by Maggie. Beth was twirling around the asymmetric bars – she spun off into a piked dismount, landed, and sprawled awkwardly on her side. So that was that. Ninety-eight per cent had not been enough. She hobbled off, supported by Miss

Amey and Dr Kennedy. Beth was out, and so, probably, were the Bush.

'Pull yourself together,' hissed Miss Amey.

'I'm sorry.' Beth wiped her eyes. 'It just hurts so much. I think I've done something really bad to it this time.'

'Don't be such a coward. I'll tell you the position once again, since your addled brain doesn't seem to grasp it. You competed on three pieces of apparatus. We aren't allowed to put the reserve in now. Either you do your exercise or we forfeit your mark. And that mark will make the difference between victory and defeat for us. Everyone else has finished. It's all up to you. Understand? Right. Put your weight on your leg. Go on. Up. How does that feel?'

Beth screamed. Her face went white; her blood might all have drained away. Miss Amey made a noise of impatience and left the room.

'Dr Kennedy, Beth wishes to try her beam exercise, but the knee is slightly painful. Could I have the anaesthetic spray? Thank you.'

Beth had thought that Miss Amey had given her up; that she was to have peace. Now here she was, back again. It was difficult to know just what was happening ... the terrible pain shooting up and down her leg like fire, the voice screaming in her ear that she was a coward, she must go back out there. Out where? Oh, the match. What match?

'Will you *listen! Beth!* I've sprayed your knee with anaesthetic. The pain should go in a moment.' Beth looked down in surprise; why, so it had. How strange. Her leg had gone away.

'Beth! Pull yourself together! What do you think we pay you for? Get on your feet. Now get out there and for

God's sake do that exercise. Do as much as you can. That bandage will hold your knee. Take the weight of the landings on the other leg. Now *go!*'

Beth wondered what the roaring noise was.

Jodie sat upright. Beth? It wasn't possible. Beth had just been carried off in agony. Oh, God, no. This was madness. No, not madness. Amey.

Beth stepped lightly up to the beam and leapt on, into a straddle position. The crowd were oddly hushed. The exercise progressed. Jodie moved closer. She saw that Beth was making slight adaptations, leaving certain things out, altering sequences of moves to favour her bad leg. It flowed smoothly; nobody not in the know would have realized. It was a masterly display of professionalism; never again would Amey be able to call Beth a gutless idiot. Jodie came nearer still, until she was able to see Beth's face – she expected grimaces, winces, even tears, but Beth looked serene and tranquil. It was like a miracle, as if a saint had touched and healed her.

The routine was almost over. Beth drew herself up, tensing for the end, readying herself for the Rostova. For a moment Jodie thought that she had decided not to do it. But then Beth gave a slight nod, almost as if she were saying – 'oh, yes, now I remember what I do' – and leapt, somersault, handspring, and then, as her knee gave way, the sickening crack of her head meeting the wood of the bar.

Mr Gurney rushed up to Miss Amey as the stretcher team vanished in the direction of the blaring ambulance siren.

'What news?'

'It's all right,' she said. 'It's all right.'

'Oh, thank God. Tell me.'

'The exercise was so nearly completed, and she managed to include so much, they're marking her for what she did, minus penalty for falling off. It was enough. We're through.'

'Thank God.'

9

The death of Beth Laurence was a tragedy, and an incalculable loss to the world of gymnastics. Mr Gurney said so, on television. Tears rolled down his plump pink cheeks as he spoke. It had been the saddest day of his life. It had been very difficult to pick up the pieces and carry on, but the effort had to be made for the sake of the other girls. He wiped his eye delicately with a monogrammed handkerchief.

The interviewer tutted sympathetically. But how had it happened?

Mr Gurney explained. Beth had been tormented by her left knee all season, but she was a girl of exceptional courage and team spirit. Her light would continue to shine in the hearts of those who had known her. Despite being helped out of the arena after damaging the knee again, she had been determined to carry on, and had insisted to the coach, Miss Amey, that the pain was not so bad that she could not attempt her beam exercise. Miss Amey had found the team doctor, explained the situation, and obtained a pain-killing spray which had been applied to the knee. Both he and Miss Amey had tried to dissuade the girl from continuing, but she had maintained that the injury was not serious, that she wanted to try. And, after all, she was the only person truly capable of judging this.

He added, after a moment, that Beth's life, though short, had been a full and rewarding one. She had brought joy to her friends and given pleasure to millions. If indeed she had to die at thirteen, he had no doubt that this was he way she would have chosen to go. Whenever he looked at his O.B.E. – he had been awarded this honour in the Birthday List, for services to gymnastics and to young people – he would be reminded of Beth. It would be as a memorial to her. It was an unspeakable tragedy. A little of his heart had frozen and died with her. It was truly terrible.

'This is terrible,' said Miss Amey. 'All we've got now is Bell. Nobody else even vaguely good on the beam. It's disastrous.'

'We should count our blessings,' Mr Gurney said piously. 'Imagine how awkward it might have been if the girl had regained consciousness before she died. Think what she might have said.'

'She might have said some very awkward things if she'd regained consciousness and *lived*. Every cloud has a silver lining.'

Mr Gurney had been reading the Bible prior to his television appearance.

'God takes care of his own,' he said thoughtfully, 'and the pounds take care of themselves. That is an excellent premise on which to run a gymnastics club, Gill. But we must work on this beam question. We will have to buy. At this stage of the season there's no alternative.'

'Nobody wants to come here,' said Miss Amey. 'I've been ringing round and putting feelers out. Not a spark of interest anywhere. I blame the Press. All this bunk about a jinx on the club, nasty innuendoes. It's wicked, frightening young girls.'

'Our own girls seem pretty shaken. It's so unprofessional. Do you realize that we've fallen to sixth in the Ambassador League? Sixth! It's a disgrace to the name of our club. We've never sunk so low. I'm not surprised if

people don't want to come here. Well, it seems that th
only thing to do is to solve the problem internally. Ther
must be some young ones we can bring along.'

'It's our only chance, isn't it?' Miss Amey said, gettin
up. 'I'll go and have a word with Lucy Maddox.'

Mrs Maddox, supervising a class of six-year-olds, wa
pleased to see Miss Amey.

'Funny you should ask that just now. Something rathe
remarkable has happened. One of the new children. Too
to the beam like a duck to water. I've seen nothing like i
since Beth . . . poor Beth. But this child – at the rate she'
progressing we could have her in the team by the tim
she's nine.'

'Do you happen to know her name?'

'I haven't got all the new girls sorted out yet, and thi
one only comes once or twice a week, but I think she sai
she was called Samantha.'

'Ah, yes. I know the one. Well, that's a lucky thing. W
have an Unborn Option on her.'

'No. Really?'

'Isn't that marvellous? There are certain domesti
problems to be overcome, though. The old story – over-
possessive mother, you know. We must toughen the gir
up – can't have her smothered. I'll suggest to Mr Gurney
that we exercise the option immediately. She can move i
here tomorrow.'

'Perhaps that would be best, Miss Amey. An Unbor
Option – what splendid news. I'll be glad of the chanc
to spend longer working with Samantha.'

'Yes,' said Miss Amey. 'Yes. And under the present cir-
cumstances it might be a good idea if I had a go at her too.

Amongst the girls there were two distinct types o
reaction; one group talked, the other was silent. Ther

was no in-between. Maggie was of the first set, Liddy of the second. The talkers sat around the Common Room table, re-hashing the fall, the events leading up to the fall, Mr Gurney's comments, one taking up where the last left off, as if afraid of what horrors their minds might conjure up, if left to silence. They could not let it rest.

Liddy sat in a corner, playing solitaire Scrabble. She appeared oblivious of the persistent voices. Her long fingers rummaged through the letters, selected, rejected, placed eight on the board, forming the words MISS AMEY. She rearranged the letters to form I'M A MESSY and contemplated this for some time.

'I can't believe it,' Liz said. 'I can't. Beth wasn't some sort of martyr. She was *finished* when they took her off. Something's wrong. She wasn't a fool.'

'You used to say she was a lunatic.'

Liz looked stunned. 'I didn't. I never said that.'

'You did.' The conversation was diverted from its main course, but soon drifted back.

'Jodie said she looked all right. She looked quite calm. Where *is* Jodie?'

'Signing books somewhere.'

'She should be here,' Liz said petulantly. Jodie had no right to go off signing books while they were talking about Beth.

Liddy chose another eight letters, and laid them in a row – MURDERER. She put this after I'M A MESSY, leaned back and gazed at the board.

'Do you think her skull was smashed?'

'SHUT UP!' Liddy turned on them, rising slowly to her feet like a caged wild animal preparing to spring. 'Shut up, shut up. What are you trying to do? Change the way it ended? How ever many times you run a piece of film the ending is always the same. Shut up. You're not helping.'

'Nor are you,' Liz said accusingly.

'Oh, stop it,' said Maggie wearily. 'It's no use attacking each other. There's nothing any of us can do.'

'Yes there is.' Liddy went to the door. 'There is something we all can do, and I'm going straight away to do it.'

Jodie stepped off the bus and began walking. It had been the most miserable afternoon. The beam stunt had been cancelled, obviously, and she had spent the two hours in utter boredom, signing her name over and over again like a machine. As a rule she enjoyed meeting the public, but today the cute, friendly smile had jarred, and she had longed to snarl and spit. Sally whispered that the smile wasn't really a good idea anyway, it did look rather unfeeling. People would understand if she looked unhappy. It might be best.

The queue had been gratifyingly long, at any rate. Sally suspected that more than a few had been drawn by morbid curiosity; they wanted a look at Beth's friend. Jodie didn't mind. She wasn't really interested. A morbidly-inspired royalty was no less than any other.

Her feet dragged with uncharacteristic heaviness. She was alone, yet she was not alone. She thought of the Church of God Everywhere. God Everywhere was a tolerable concept; Beth Everywhere was not. Oh, what *did* happen to the dead? Could Beth see her now? And, worse, could Beth see inside her head? This tormented Jodie from sunrise to nightfall. Her every thought was followed by – does Beth know I'm thinking this? And so many of her thoughts ... well, she really wouldn't want Beth to know them. She tried hard to shut down her thinking processes altogether, to blank her mind, but learned that this was an impossibility.

Eventually she allowed herself to reach the comforting

conclusion that Beth might be Anywhere, but not Everywhere, not at the same time. It was possible that Beth could choose to read her mind for a while, now and then, but unlikely that she would stay there for long. She would move on to more interesting places, to her family.

She shivered, remembering the funeral and the haunting sight of those two people – the woman, white, haggard, looking about fifty – she'd always thought Beth's mother much younger than that – and the tiny girl at her side, clutching her hand, eyes huge, round and scared. That was where Beth would be. With them.

She trailed on, past Bagnall's, in through the side gate, and halted abruptly, for the rest of the team were all leaning out of the window, waving urgently at her with such animation that for a moment she truly believed that they would tell her that Beth was back, and hadn't it all been a marvellous joke?

'But that's illegal. You can't.'

'We can and we have,' said Maggie. 'And we've all rung our parents to tell them to fetch us tonight. I've packed already. John Phillips is leaving too. He loved Beth.'

'But walking out on a contract? He'll sue.' Jodie rocked thoughtfully from one foot to the other.

Maggie laughed scornfully. 'What – take a load of kids to court? I can just see it. He'd be a laughing stock. One of us perhaps, but not all. Solidarity, that's the thing. There's strength in numbers. United we stand.' Not for nothing was Maggie the daughter of a shop steward. She had taken over and organized the walkout with the cool firm hand of experience; Maggie had celebrated her fifth birthday sitting on a picket line.

'Tell her about the Press.'

'We've issued a statement. The entire team is walking

out as a demonstration against Gurney's cover-up. We don't believe his story. Not a word of it. This is the only way to get the publicity we need. He's *not* going to lie his way out of murder.'

Tracy Wilcox appeared at the door.

'He's asking for you, Jodie.'

'Go on, kid. Give him what for. Get him where it hurts.' Maggie slapped Jodie on the back. As she walked away from them she heard Liddy's voice begin to sing:

> 'We shall be avenged,
> We shall be avenged . . .'

to the tune of 'We shall overcome', and the whole team took it up, their voices rising with determination –

> 'We shall be avenged for Beth . . .'

'Silly children,' said Mr Gurney. 'That's all they are you know. Children. I don't know what they hope to achieve by this.'

'Will you go to court over the contracts?' Jodie asked.

'Hardly. Why publicize their ridiculous accusations? This will all have blown over within a week or so. Just another nine-day wonder.'

'A walkout by the entire team?' Her voice was scornful.

'I'm afraid they aren't as important as they'd like to think. They will learn their lesson. They're banging the nails in their own coffins, not in mine. They're unemployable. Contract-breakers. No other club can sign them up. Such a waste of promising careers.' He shrugged. 'Financial suicide.'

Jodie said nothing. God, but she despised him.

'It's a fortunate piece of timing that the news of my O.B.E. should have come through just now. I think the Queen's opinion is the one that carries weight, don't you?

I've always realized that you were something rather different, Jodie. You have the mind of an adult, not of a silly emotional adolescent. We can build up a great team here; I as manager, you as captain. We have a fine pool of up-and-coming talent, and the season is by no means dead – we're still in Europe, a fourth round tic in Rome ... Of course, you will be the cement that holds the new team together. You are vital. Therefore, I feel it only right to offer you a considerable increase in salary.'

He named a figure more than three times as large as her current wage. He's desperate, thought Jodie. I'm the last hope of a desperate man. She laughed aloud. He had underestimated her. If he thought Jodie Bell could be so easily corrupted, he was in for a very unpleasant shock.

Derek was the first reporter to arrive, running headlong through the doorway in a obvious state of wild excitement.

'Jodie! This is just fantastic, darling. You're doing a marvellous thing.'

'Do you think so?'

'You bet. I was there, you know, at that match. I saw the whole business – I was never happy about it. Never. I agree with what you're saying. That vile Amey woman was behind the whole thing ...'

'I'm staying,' said Jodie.

'... and I'm damned if I'm not going to find a way to prove it.'

'*Derek*. I'm staying.' The eventual price of Jodie's corruption had been double Mr Gurney's original offer. Already she was wondering if she had made a serious mistake. So shaken had he been, she might just have been able to force him higher. His hand had been trembling most fascinatingly as he signed the contract.

team. What do you mean?'

'The whole team except me. You'll never prove anything, Derek. Nobody was there in the dressing-room. Nobody knows. I can't see anything wrong with what Mr Gurney says. I believe him.'

Derek gazed at her, long and hard.

'How much did he pay you, Jodie?'

'I don't know what you mean. But, Derek . . .'

He hesitated briefly, then turned and began to walk towards the door where Maggie, Liddy and the team were gathered with their suitcases.

'Derek! Come back. Where are you going?'

'To talk to some human beings.'

'Oh, Derek, listen. Listen to what I'm saying. There's not . . .'

'Sorry. I really don't want to know.' He sounded bored. 'Oh – and you can have my share of the royalties. Your need is much, much greater than mine.'

Maggie waved at him as he approached, eager to tell their story. Jodie watched, slightly puzzled; there was a pain in her side, but it was nothing that she recognized, and she expected that it would soon go away.

ONE MORE RIVER
Lynne Reid Banks

Life in Canada had always been safe and happy for Lesley
Shelby, but then her father announced that they were going
to Israel, and everything changed. This is the story of their
hard new life in the Kibbutz on the banks of the River
Jordan, and of the stresses and strains of her secret friendship
with an Arab boy whose loyalty to his people is at war with his
love for her.

MISCHLING, SECOND DEGREE
Ilse Koehn

Ilse Koehn was six years old in 1935 when, unknown to her,
she became a Mischling, Second Degree citizen in Nazi
Germany because her grandmother was Jewish. Her family
kept the secret from her, but as the war closed in on Germany
she sensed that there was some vague danger, some secret in
her past, but it was not until she was 15 that she came to know
the truth.

THE WRITING ON THE WALL
Lynne Reid Banks

Kev is a bad influence – or at least that's what Tracy's dad
thinks – so she isn't surprised when her parents won't let her
go on holiday with him alone. But Tracy is determined to
have some fun before she has to settle down in a boring job
like her sister. So she finds a good way of getting round her
dad – at least, it seems a good way at the time ...

THE PIGMAN'S LEGACY
Paul Zindel

Consumed with guilt and grief since the death of Mr Pignati John and Lorraine determine to help another old man they find in his abandoned house. They force their way into his life, full of plans to make amends for their past mistakes, but things go very wrong and they begin to wonder if the Pigman's legacy is simply too much for them to handle.

A QUEST FOR ORION
Rosemary Harris

Fleeing from the terror of the Freaks, who have overrun and enslaved Western Europe, Jan and her friends realize that their only hope for freedom is to fight back. An exciting but disturbing tale of a future world dominated by barbarians.

EMPTY WORLD
John Christopher

Neil Miller is alone after the death of his family in an accident. So when a virulent plague sweeps across the world dealing death to all it touches, Neil has a double battle for survival: not just for the physical necessities of life but with the subtle pressures of fear and loneliness.